A Purinton

Autumn leaves

a collection of poems

A Purinton

Autumn leaves
a collection of poems

ISBN/EAN: 9783337374723

Printed in Europe, USA, Canada, Australia, Japan

Cover: Foto ©Andreas Hilbeck / pixelio.de

More available books at **www.hansebooks.com**

AUTUMN LEAVES.

A COLLECTION OF POEMS

BY

A. PURINTON.

LYNN, MASS., 1886.

SALEM, MASS.:

OBSERVER BOOK AND JOB PRINT,

1886.

DEDICATION.

TO

JULIA ANN BOYCE,

AND

OTHER DEAR FRIENDS

Who have encouraged me in publishing

AUTUMN LEAVES,

THIS BOOK IS DEDICATED

With the love and best wishes of the Author.

Preface.

The author begs leave to explain to those who read these pages, that her advanced age of more than "three-score years and ten," found her accepting the advice of friends to publish these poems, most of which were written years ago, without the least expectation of putting them before a critical public. She asks all to be charitable in their criticisms, remembering the book is published with the hope of gaining a competence to help secure a comfortable home during the few days of life which may remain to her.

LYNN, MASS., NOV. 22, 1886.

TABLE OF CONTENTS.

OLD LYNN.

In by-gone days within our reach,
A winding path led to the beach.
I have pleasant memories still
Of the Salt Works, and old Wind Mill.

And now, it might seem rather harsh
To pick our way over the old salt marsh ;
Carefully stepping o'er hillock and stones,
At the fearful risk of breaking our bones.

Or making a detour far and wide,
Lest we slip in the slime pools left by the tide ;
And our mothers, we'd not dare to meet,
With muddy frocks and dripping feet.

But all these dangers safely passed,
And our crowning wish secured at last,
We went rejoicing on our way,
To " Sagamore Hill " around by the bay.

And we climbed up the green hill's brow,
Where there's nothing but streets and houses now :
And where the hill was dug away
Are found the houses of to-day.

2

But grazing on the sides so green,
The cows in pastures might be seen.
While a few old houses brown and gray,
Were sprinkled all along the way.

What would some of the old folk say,
Could they see the city of to-day!
Flaming in colors gay and bright,
Glowing in the electric light.

One sweet June day, I was beguiled
Into fresh pastures green and wild,
And up the steep hills sloping side,
Where tangled vines the mosses hide,

Our footsteps turned to that famed spot
In the deep woods, Old Dungeon Rock ;
Scarce tempted by the bright array
Of flowers upspringing on our way,

We hastened on, up the wild slopes,
To the crowning Mecca of our hopes ;
And feeling ourselves greatly blessed,
Reaching at last that place of rest.

Tradition says that Captain Kid
His immense treasure here had hid :
And it was said an earthquake's shock
Had shattered and disturbed the rock.

And it may be we held our cosy chat
In the very same place the robber sat
And counted his ill-gotten gains,
Ere burying them with so much pains.

And repeated the story old,
By my grandmother so often told,
As with garrulous and dulcet tones
She talked of the old ancestral homes.

It was in the good old times he went,
In Salem's earlier settlement,
And, as I judge from her report,
Great uncle, or something of that sort.

And left one heart so true and tried
Who sought in vain her grief to hide ;
And hope and faith alike grew dim,
As she never heard one word from him.

Her bounding heart its hopes renew,
Whene'er a ship's sail caught her view ;
But no tidings came of any sort,
From any ship that came in port.

So time went on ; after some years
Strange rumors aggravate her fears ;
Her hopes deferred and feverish grown,
She to an early grave went down.

While his ship, the sport of every breeze,
At last the cruel Pirates seize;
And powerless with this bandit horde
Are murdered and thrown overboard.

But he, of all the crew was left,
And into useful service pressed;
Roving the seas from clime to clime,
And never joining them in crime.

As their chances of escape grew less,
And sick of this life of wretchedness,
They conned among themselves the plan
Whether to kill or save the man.

They drew from him such solemn oaths,
Never their secret to disclose;
Directing him to a secret spot
Where buried treasures might be got.

And for his life's sake he must say
No other one should learn the way.
In the meanest lives of sin and shame,
Some thoughts of justice will remain.

Finding on his returning home,
That love and joy for him were gone:
He lived alone, and while others slept,
From prying eyes his secret kept.

And how he went, or when he came,
Must ever be to them the same.
And when the fogs hung thick and low,
Off in his little boat he'd go.

And it may be, came round the bay,
And through the thickets found his way.
On through the woods to this same spot,
And here his buried treasures sought.

With no one but himself to please,
He could like Indians mark the trees.
And this accounts for his odd ways,
Oft being gone for several days.

The Marbles thought by the spirits' aid
That they could find where it was laid.
And here they dug an immense cave,
About which all the people rave.

They dug by night, they dug by day,
But from their digging came no pay ;
For all the money which they got,
Was from the crowd that thronged the spot.

LYNN AT PRESENT.

Its sunny hills and rustic vales
    Are open to the sea,
Upon whose beach the crested waves
    Roll grandly wild and free.

And hundreds make it a resort
    In sunshine and in showers,
Liking, with the wild waves, to sport
    Away their leisure hours,

Or, by an eager wish spurred on,
    In spite of wind and wave,
Some visit the old "Spouting Horn,"
    And view the "Swallows' Cave."

There one may take such airy flights,
    On fancy's sportive wings,
And revel in the pure delight
    Imagination brings.

And would you settle down in Lynn,
    Resolved to take your chance,
You'll find along with rush and din,
    They steadily advance.

There may be found the opulent,
    The learned, and the wise ;

Some of more active temperament,
  And those who seek to rise.

The merchant and mechanic,
  Prolific streams from whence
The nation draws her tonic,
  Giving health and strength.

And there are open to the wise,
  Who find them, more or less,
With energy and enterprise,
  Roads leading to success.

For with this close alliance
  Of steam and telegram,
They have every appliance,
  Which does not prove a sham.

And as I looked around,
  This inference I drew,
That where so many do abound,
  There must be suffering too.

Standing aloof, yet not apart,
  In numbers not a few,
Are those who seek with all their heart,
  The Master's work to do.

No matter where you do belong,
  So many churches wait,

Ready to take you right along,
  E'en up to Heaven's gate.

And you must ever bear in mind,
  If your way is not quite clear,
That all the isms with their kind,
  Are getting less severe.

And 'neath the temples sanctified
  By penitence and prayer,
The noble charities reside,
  And raise their altars there.

The Sunday schools and libraries.
  Like magic, diffuse peace,
And the humane societies
  Are ever on the increase.

The mighty import of a thought,
  That struggles into life,
May coming destinies involve,
  With future interests rife.

Pity to fling away a thought
  In eager search for gold,
Since all its purchased pleasures soon
  Must leave the heart so cold.

Granted it is the talisman
  Without which all soon fails ;

There needs must be a steady hand
   To balance well the scales.

The hospitals are open wide
   To all whose wants appeal ;
The antidotes are well supplied,
   With soothing balm to heal.

If you go down North Common street,
   I'll readily engage
You'll find a safe and sure retreat
   For poverty and age.

Where want and sorrow pressing sore
   Gave no respite to care :
Their burdens dropping at the door,
   They find a refuge there.

And there are others, not a few,
   By the highest instincts led ;
Their ministries distil like dew,
   Rich blessings on their head.

The fair for the Old Ladies' Home,
   Which seems to be their forte,
Was thought by those who go and come,
   A triumph of high art.

It was viewed with admiration,
   As a wonder of its kind,

A perfect inspiration
  Of the creative mind.

While offerings, so freely showered,
  A halo o'er them flings,
So like the precious ointment poured,
  A savor of good things.

May blessings spring in their pathway,
  With roseate hues be fraught,
That sparkle like the diamonds ray,
  With the rich gems of thought.

God bless the men and women too,
  Who in these charities engage,
And may both loving hearts and true
  Reward them in old age

To some I am sure my story
  Were more than half forgot,
Without its crowning glory,
  The eminence High Rock.

Who that has climbed its dizzy height
  And viewed the prospect over,
Be filled with pleasure and delight
  At the ocean and the shore.

How grandly with each changing hue
    Does the rich landscape gleam
With its wondrous far stretching view
    Of forest, hill and stream.

Or in the highlands overlook
    Those beautiful abodes
That on shady hill or sunny nook
    Seemed clad in gala robes.

While coming forth on every hand,
    Fresh as the morning dew,
There little ones, a smiling band,
    In charming beauty grew.

JESSIE LEE.

Our fathers sought for freedom,
    But they often turned aside,
For with election and probation
    Their hearts were sorely tried.

The vicious and debased
　　Alike were tempest-tossed ;
For how could any one be saved
　　That was destined to be lost ?

And one disheartning feature
　　About which the fathers raved,
Was, that our poor human nature
　　Seemed so utterly depraved.

This led to much disscusion—
　　Doubting, fear and strife,
Poisoning the very atmosphere
　　Of a true and higher life.

That they wrestled with transgression,
　　And sought for peace and rest,
Is but a dim suggestion,
　　Of their highest, noblest, best.

With vengeful spirit underneath,
Quakers were hunted down to death,
And it may be that all too soon
Persistence hastened on their doom.

For who would ever dare intrude
Upon his self-sought solitude :
Or mar by any social strife,
The promptings of his inner life.

And could such violence be done
Had they kept meditating on ?
They felt expedients so rash,
The hangman's cord, the whip, and lash.

Still further adding to their woes,
By Rawson shipped to Barbadoes ;
Drawn on by passions so irate
To give expression to their hate.

Close wedded to their forms and creeds,
They seemed unconscious of their deeds.
And mammon with his lordly pride,
And pomp, and state, were deified.

The great need of that trying hour
Was kind help from a higher power.
From doubt and darkness into light,
To redeem them from their sorry plight.

Already there was in the field
A torch from Wesley and Whitfield.
An Angel of mercy we shall see,
Came in the person of Jessie Lee.

And the scoffers' laugh and priestly sneers
Fell like chaff on believers' ears.
And the thorns and briars which good seed choke,
Vanished at once in fire and smoke.

And fired with the flames of a new advent,
On to Boston the Preacher went.
Fearing naught in his holy quest,
No one to trouble or molest.

And still whate'er his going forth,
Or living evidence of worth,
Or work for souls he had in mind.
To no church, entrance could he find. '

No altar waited him to bring
A message from the Great High King ;
No roof above but the translucent sky,
And its star-spangled canopy.

But He who calls them each by name.
His garment spreads o'er all the same,
While they obeying His command
Rest in the hollow of His hand.

The Master being at the helm,
He straightway went to the old Elm ;
And, being drawn by the sweet sounds,
A goodly number gathered round.

They lingered near to hear him tell
Of Jesus at Samaria's well.
The old, old story, ever new
For those who thirst and hunger too.

And, seeing many by the way,
Continued there to sing and pray,
On the common, a sweet, lovely spot,
Where all who chose could go or not.

And while they lingered as if spell-bound.
A feeling of distrust went round.
And not a soul among them dared
To offer him a shelter unprepared.

While some waxed warm with good intent,
Still others were on mischief bent.
And doubtless much good seed was sown,
Where wheat and tares had together grown.

Sadly he turned himself about ;
Hungry and cold, he was left out ;
O, what could more his feelings rasp
Than this disdain, thus o'er him cast !

He searched his pocket, and from thence
Took only thirty-seven cents,
And saw with this he must contrive
To keep both man and horse alive.

And can we wonder if he doubt
The mission which had called him out ?
It must be so ; here was no cheat,
Satan was sifting him like wheat.

And would he, could he stand the test,
Like doubting Thomas at the best?
'Twas but one moment, only one,
No real mischief could be done.

If self be nailed unto the cross,
Could he not suffer pain and loss?
And this might only be the test;
He would follow on to know the rest.

But as the night was setting in
An invitation came from Lynn,
Which Satan's forces set to route,
And man and horse at once set out.

The wild waves rushed with deafening roar,
O'er the salt marsh along the shore.
The road being rough and incomplete,
Scarred in passing, the horse's feet.

A rift of light, one glimmering ray.
Shot from the light-house o'er the bay,
And snow and hail with blinding force
An impetus gave to man and horse.

On he drove through the keen, cold air;
His soul uplifted in praise and prayer,
For in himself he was a host
Moved by the power of the Holy Ghost.

It may have been from tongues of flame,
That into his soul the Spirit came ;
And gave him that foretaste of heaven,
Which Paul and Silas had in prison.

He hastened on ; an hour or more
Brought him to Mr. Johnson's door,
And, filled with joy, he found at last,
Glad welcome and the warm hand-clasp.

The light, the warmth, the genial glow
Of Christian fellowship below ;
And such a feast ! it might have been
Enough to satisfy a king.

And then, as if the feast to crown,
The Master's blessing is called down.
And O, with what supreme delight
He held a meeting that very night.

And the next day in the forenoon,
Another in the great front room.
And how, as if by magic sent
So many people came and went.

For the preacher, now being housed,
To special efforts was aroused,
And ministered in words and deeds
To all their spiritual needs.

4

And as if the emergency to meet,
His zeal was kindled to white heat.
Until it seemed to him almost
There was camping round a mighty host.

Pilgrim and stranger though he came,
Known only to them by his name,
Yet of such wondrous power possessed,
He captured all that he addressed.

His eyes so mild, with fire seemed lit
As he proclaimed from holy writ ;
He awakened such a faith in some,
Persuading them to Christ to come.

There were some who drank life's bitter cup
Who, with faith renewed, looked calmly up.
And some poor wrecks of shame and sin,
From ways of darkness, were drawn in.

And some poor victims of the fall,
Came readily and gave up all.
The oneness of his end and aim,
Their close attention seemed to gain.

The fruits of this new sensation
    Were seen in a little church
Which after two weeks in building,
    Was finished even to the porch.

Their hearts with joy elate,
  Broke forth in gladsome song,
And burst the bonds of fate
  That had fettered them so long.

No organ lent its thrilling tones
  To the trained choir above,
But none the less did praise ascend
  From hearts attuned by love.

The summer airs were laden
  With sweet scents from fields,
With the song of birds, and matins
  Which bounteous nature yields.

But there were the gleam of sunshine ;
  And the gentle stir of the breeze ;
The waving of the branches ;
  And the rustling of the leaves.

  What need of paint or fresco,
When in the sun's bright shine
  Could be clearly traced the pattern
Of flower and leaf and vine ?

And for the work hereafter,
  A pastor must be found ;
Willing to plant and water,
  And it might be, till the ground.

And filled with love for the master,
  Which kindled to a flame,
While looking to the future,
  On Bishop Asbury came.

Although small the little church,
  And smaller yet the fee,
Yet all the same the edifice
  Must dedicated be.

His fervent Apostolic zeal,
  Merging in plans so broad,
All emanated from a life
  Hidden with Christ in God.

Deep calling unto deep,
  In his Prophetic soul ;
Before him as on a sea of glass
  The future lies unrolled.

He said that from that hour
  An influence should go forth,
That, reaching out from east to west,
  Should rouse the South and North.

He fathomed the abyss
  Of wretchedness and sin,
Which, serpent-like, had coiled round,
  And was dragging them within

And as his ravished soul
  The vision passed before,
He saw a countless throng arise
  Like sands on the sea-shore ;

Struggling as if for life,
  On the incoming wave,
Freighted with souls of priceless worth
  Which Christ alone could save.

And by the tragic wail
  From this prison-house of sin,
He saw the soil was ready
  To put the ploughshare in.

And seeing eye to eye,
  From the beginning to the close,
He felt the tangled wilderness
  Would blossom like the rose.

And from the whitened fields,
  Would float upon the breeze,
The sound of reapers coming home,
  Bearing along their sheaves.

BY-GONES.

As, by soft winds are gently stirred
   The ripples on a lake,
So even a slight or careless word,
   The silent memories wake.

And if the hidden memories start,
   So long in silence lain,
To lacerate the aching heart,
   With all their torturing pain ;

'Twere better far to heave the sigh
   O'er thoughts of long ago,
Than 'neath their shattered casement lie,
   Of apathy and woe.

Those shattered chords may ne'er respond
   To love's sweet dream again,
Or listen to those accents fond,
   Whose utterances were vain.

Quite vain were words to liken
   This new joy which o'er me broke
When, to the measure of its bliss,
   The heart responsive woke;

And joyful thrills ecstatic, did o'er
    My heart strings play,
Like a beautiful strain of music,
    That softly steals away.

So like the gold and amber hues,
    That gild the clouds of even ;
As bright and evanescent too,
    Just on the verge of heaven.

In sighs the fond heart sought relief ;
    Its tears in secret wept ;
And o'er the ashes of its grief,
    Its nightly vigils kept.

Upspringing from the smouldering heap,
    That now in ruin lies,
Where love and grief their vigils keep,
    Shall faith and hope arise.

For angels with their spotless wings,
    Are fanning into life
That evidence of unseen things,
    With wondrous power, so rife.

The disenchanted soul looks up
    With eager, longing eyes ;
The angel of the golden cup
    It readily descrys.

The golden nectar it distills
　　Is full and sparkling o'er
And thou mayst even drink thy fill
　　And yet there still is more.

THE POETRY IN NATURE.

'Tis said, somewhere, a mighty spirit broods
In secret haunts among the grand old woods ;
Pierces the sod, strikes at the hidden roots,
And pushes into life the little shoots.
In endless changes, its transforming power
Produces stem and leaf, then bud and flower.
In all the earth, the sky, the sea, the air,
An unseen spirit dwelleth everywhere.
In heights sublime, in forms of perfect grace,
In storms and calms, upon the ocean's face ;
A subtle essence without form or name,
That shines in light and glows in living flame ;
That reappears in forms, forever strange and new;

And gives to color its transcendent hue :
Blending in forms and shapes of every size,
The finer shades with those of deeper dyes.
I fain would seek among the woodland shades,
In sunny slopes, or on the rocky glades ;
It may be lingering in some grassy dell,
Among those scenes that shepherds love so well.
Or is the tangled greenwood its retreat,
Where gay wood-nymphs and fairies ofttimes meet ?
Or, in the mountains' bold and craggy steeps,
While lesser sprites along with lichens creep ?
The little ant showeth her instincts well,
And babbling brooks would fain these secrets tell.
Of warbling birds, it may be thou art king,
Whose sweet vocation is to soar and sing.
Say, dost thou people all the earth and air,
And now art here, and art thou everywhere ?
In sparry caves, the sea-nymphs love to rove :
Or deeper yet among the coral groves,
Where sparkle gems, that mock the sun's bright ray,
And glittering diamonds pave the floorless way.
Mayhap in fairy grot or sylvan glen,
Or caverned depths ne'er visited by men:
In whose recess no ray of sunlight falls,
Or slumbering echoes answer to the calls ;
Whose spacious halls formed in the solid rock,
And vaulted roof by heavy columns propped,

In vastness, grandeur, and stupendous plan,
The work of ages, were it done by man.
On every hand, by kindly nature reared,
Fantastic forms of birds and flowers appeared ;
While living founts send forth their cooling spray,
And soft cascades go murmuring on their way.
While the rich pendants hanging from the wall,
In crystal drops from icy globules fall ;
And grotesque figures crested o'er with spray,
In mailed coats seem starting on their way.
It maybe that awhile all nature slept ;
Forth from those caves, the giant mountains leapt,
And lifting up their solemn heads on high,
N'er rested till their summits reached the sky.
Their patient heads wrapped in a snowy shroud,
Girded by sunbeams, draped in snowy clouds ;
While sailing slowly round their craggy steep,
The lowering clouds in teary raindrops weep ;
And when the fearful elements assail,
Folding their heads within a misty veil,
Yet firm, undaunted, braving every shock,
Themselves unmoved while dread convulsions rock ;
Dumb, voiceless orators, ye silent stand,
Raised monuments, by an Almighty Hand. '
Speechless, yet speaking ever to the eye
Of the majestic grandeur throned on high.
No small fatigue, no danger mean, or light,

Attends the traveller up that dizzy height.
Fairly equipped, with guide and wholesome fare,
Choosing the safest route with proper care ;
The first ascent always so pleasant made,
By spicy gales wafted from flowery glade,
While mountain nymphs, or bolder huntsman's horn,
The mirthful echoes wilder yet prolong.
As now the traveller leaves the dewy vales,
A more invigorating atmosphere inhales.
Ascending up the bold and rugged steep,
His mule abandoned, oft obliged to creep
Around a precipice, whose lofty brow
Hangs o'er the yawning abyss, deep below ;
And yet such frightful chasms must be passed,
At the bare thought of which, we stand aghast.
Adown whose depths, seeming extended wide,
No slanting rays of sunbeams ever glide.
Where reptile forms of giant monsters brood,
Alike the scourge and terror of the good,
He ventures on ; his safety ne'er consults ;
Each fresh endeavor bringing good results ;
Until at last, emboldened by success,
The task seems lighter and the danger lies.
Yet even a fragment loosed, or rolling stone,
Would hurl him downward into depths unknown.
He glances upward ; every nerve is strained ;
With aching limbs, and swollen-to-bursting veins,

His practised eye, by no weak fears assailed,
A foothold gains, where timorous ones have failed ;
Worn with fatigue, and daylight near its close,
He yields at last to quiet and repose.
Midst purple tints and gold and amber hues,
The God of day slowly retiring views ;
Admiring from that eminence so high,
The brilliancy of the translucent sky ;
Viewing with strange and marvelous delight
The wondrous hangings of the curtained night.
His soul goes forth in deep research alone,
In intense longings for the great unknown.
Among the stars he revels in his flight,
And basks in the effulgence of their light.
In reverence, listens to that voice divine,
The sacred presence of the inner shrine :
The infant seer that oft in silence waits
Upon the Priestess that devines our fate ;
That nestles in behind each fear and doubt,
And dares to hunt the lurking demons out ;
Those petted minions of our love and hate,
That in disguise upon the passions wait.
A deeper consciousness within is born,
Intensely glowing as that radiant morn.
The misty haze that round the mountain sails,
Is slowly lifting its transparent veils.
And sylph-like forms, seem graceful, bending low,

To crown with garlands its majestic brow.
He reaches heights immeasurably grand ;
Beyond is stretching vast extents of land,
Whose cities, watered by full many a stream,
Like miniatures upon the landscape gleam.
Across the valley's gorge, from left to right,
Is stretched a solid floor of dazzling white.
On either hand, the lofty glaciers rise,
Their form and number, various as their size.
Their silent, calm, and yet continuous flow,
Freshens and beautifies the vales below.
The gelid mass to such consistence glued,
Midst fine clad hills, and flowery slopes protrude.
The snow-clad gorges, wreathed in glittering white,
Dazzles to blindness the strained and aching sight.
The Heavens are bowed, and seem so very near ;
The rose-tint clouds like seraph forms appear.
Their softened hues together sweetly blend,
And all the magic of enchantment lend.
What sudden transports seize the enraptured mind,
While gazing from these alpine heights sublime.
The woodland hills, each soft and dewy plain,
Seem to recede and then advance again.
Ecstatic wonder looks from out his face,
Viewing the vast immensity of space.
And mightier still the ocean's rolling flood,
The vaulted heavens, and over all is God.

RETROSPECTION.

Come back, come back, my youthful hours!
  Why flee away so fast?
Bring out from memory's hidden cells,
  Sweet visions of the past.

When roaming on the sandy beach,
  I watched the heaving sea,
Or liked the winged sea-bird, with
  The wild waves sported free.

Who would not wish to cherish
  The joys too pure to last?
Or linger o'er the ashes
  Of those blossoms of the past?

When entering on life's flowery vales
  Fresh with the dew of youth,
With all its joyous freedom,
  Its innocence and truth.

O, happy days of gay romance,
  Ye never seemed too long!
For then the joyous soul went forth
  In melody and song.

All gushing o'er with happiness,
  And full of careless glee,
I asked or knew not why it was;
  It was joy enough *to be.*

I little dreamed the fevered flush,
  The bright illusive glow,
Was but the prelude to a life
  Of sorrow and of woe.

No shadow of the coming years
  A sadness o'er us cast ;
I only knew my present joys
  Were fleeing all too fast.

But later still the heart has learned,
  What some may sooner see,
That every added cup of joy
  Must drugged with poison be.

And vain must be the cherished hope,
  So fondly pondered o'er,
That fate may have a sunnier spot,
  Than those we hold in store.

For scarcely could we spare an hour
  To win the soft control,
Or feel the renovating power,
  That elevates the soul.

Nestling within their quiet depths,
  The hidden mem'ries lie,
Ready to start at the slightest touch
  Of the rude passer-by.

THE SNOW.

Fairylike fleeting, thou fallest from above,
Emblem of innocence, beauty and love.
Riding the winds, in all thy mad mirth.
Wildly careering o'er all the fair earth.

Crystal and dewdrop come huryring past,
Driven along by the dark mountain blast.
Gracefully eddying, whirling around,
Falling so gently all over the ground.

Strange are the thoughts our bosoms now fill,
Watching the storm king pass by at his will,
Robing the valley and decking the heath,
Crowning the trees with a bright, snowy wreath.

Beautiful snowflake, in all thy wild mirth,
Emblem of innocence, purity, mirth.
Why hast thou come from the place of thy birth
To tarnish thy beauty by contact with earth.

THE OLD AND THE NEW.

What if the devotee of rites monastic,
 Her gorgeous scenes parade before our eyes,
Midst the improvements of the age scholastic,
 From burning censors, fumes of incense rise.
No longer now, as in the time of olden,
 No border minstrels pipe their lofty strains
Of castle, hall, or tower, or palace golden ;
 Naught but the crumbling ruin now remains.

Yet in the forests of those old dominions,
 The solitary night bird sings alone,
The snowy swan with smooth. unruffled pinion,
 On the calm waters of the lake moves down,
Where slumbering lie the hords of memories an-
  tique,
 The gathered heaps of legendary lore.
Unroll the volume of an age pedantic,
 With fragmentary truth all scattered o'er.

Aye with a pen dipped as with living fire,
 Oil from the crucible upon it turn,
And as the lambent flames rise higher, higher,
 Let thoughts that live, upon its surface burn.
The lettered word upon its pages glowing,
 As stars gleam out upon a dusky night,
A clear and bright illumined pathway showing,
 The way worn wanderer leading to the light.
6

The holier fragments of mediæval culture,
    The fainter echoes of a far off day,
Are the foreshadowings of a glorious future,
    Whose morn is brightened by its dawning ray.
If now beneath their lofty shadows glooming,
    Of gothic aisle in dim cathedral vast,
Do organ tones in solemn anthem swelling,
    A sombre shadow o'er the spirit cast.

No longer are the gentle airs of heaven,
    Disturbed by Autumn's low gutterial wail,
Now with the hymn are sweeter strains inwoven,
    In solemn pauses dying on the gale.
Those heavenly tones hushed to a deeper stillness,
    Broken by wintry gusts come sweeping past
In sadder strains, leaving an icy chillness,
    Into a deeper silence hushed at last.

The soul prepared, a higher bliss partaking,
    To midnight chants succeeds the song of praise,
Responsively new melodies awakening.
    In rapturous notes, or choral hymn of praise.
Joy to the soul, that gazes from the headland,
    Upon the golden city bathed in light,
In the dim distance glances at the inland,
    Slowly receding from its eager sight.

As near the footstool of the cross approaching,
    It views the grandeur of the sacrifice,

The new-born soul in pæans of rejoicing,
　Flow ceaseless forth in music harmonies,
Of summer airs, there was a breath so vernal,
　The springing buds into existence haste,
Giving a promise of a growth perennial,
　Of flowers upspringing in the wintry waste.

THE FLIGHT OF TIME.

Another year has come and gone,
Bearing us silently along,
The winged Angel in his flight,
Sped like an arrow from our sight.

And where are all our hopes and fears,
And visions of the coming years.
Our sorrows, joys, and wishes gone,
In the swift current borne along?

And oh! how many a smile and tear,
Have mingled with the by-gone year,
And sighs that rend the heart in twain,
Have mingled in one clustering train.

Ah! smiling spring, and leafy June,
And summer flowers fade all too soon,
Blossoms so bright, beyond compare,
Leave naught but fragrance on the air.

And gone with the departing year,
Are sounds of music, mirth, and cheer,
And dance, and revelry, and songs,
Have led their votaries along.

And mingled with its music tones
Are solemn, hushed, and deep, low moans :
For youth and beauty in its bloom,
Low gathered to the silent tomb.

Those soft, low tones, so sweet and clear,
Still linger on the listening ear,
The last mild, tender, sad farewell ;
The sable hearse, and funeral knell,

So mournfully sweep o'er the soul,
Like lava tides that onward roll,
The recollections light and clear,
As scenes long vanished, reappear.

Stay, winged time! O, why so fast,
Our record bearing of the past,
The mighty past, 'tis gone, O where,
And echo answers, where, Oh! where.

The past, the past, the vanished past,
A dim foreboding o'er us cast,
Its fleeting glories seem to say,
So surely you must pass away.

MUSIC.

Aye, strike thy harp, yes, strike once again,
And let it breathe a soul-subduing strain,
As rising clear it softly steals along,
Swelling into a cadence rich and strong.

At closing day the sun recedes from sight
Millions of dew-drops flashing back the light,
O'er verdant hill and mead the insect throng
Pour a rich flood of melody along.

In the dim distance on its shadowy way,
'Tis floating past, a sweet and plaintive lay,
On the winged air by mortals never trod,
It bears the soul up to the throne of God.

WINTER.

The earth a chilly aspect wears,
  All carpeted with snow,
And yet it warms and giveth life
  To the sweet buds below.
For scarcely has it taken
  Its departure from the earth,
Ere all the tender nurslings
  Come springing into birth.
At the chill wind and biting frost.
  We hastily exclaim,
Yet how it sends the warm life blood,
  On tingling through the veins.
Behold upon the window panes,
  What myriad forms are seen,
In countless swarms of birds, and flowers,
  Forming an icy screen.
How fearless are the elements,
  When riding on the blast,
With the majesty of conquest,
  The storm king rushes past.
We gather near the loved ones.
  With pale and anxious look,
And doubly blessed is the charm
  Of music or of book.

THE SONG OF LIFE.

Ah whether it be of care or pleasure,
Life is set to tuneful measure ;
Some it may be fast or slow,
Set to a key too high or low ;
Whether it be of care or pleasure,
Life is set to tuneful measure.

Some on whom the fates have smiled
Dance through life a joyous child,
Others a long and mournful train,
Step to a sadder, milder strain ;
Yet whether it be of high or low,
Swift or strong or soft or slow,
Whether it be of pain or pleasure,
Life is set to tuneful measure.

Some 'neath this load of care and woe
Walk to measures painfully slow,
Others again, and many there be,
Step to a nobler strain and free ;
Some there are of the merry throng,
Whose gay young life is a summer song,
They flutter about for a few short hours,
Then fade away like the summer flowers.

Sad, alas ! yet all too true,
Causing discords not a few,
Are the broken strings that oft are wrung,
From shattered chords that are all unstrung ;
Oh! the thoughtless, reckless, wild,
With youth and truth and virtue soiled.

Dancing without fear or strife,
O'er the precipices of life,
Those to truth and honor false,
Along in the giddy waltz ;
Theirs the swift and airy flights,
O'er folly's mazy heights.

Since their steps have downward led,
All their fair young promise fled,
Dashing thoughtlessly along,
See them join the merry throng ;
Dancing, prancing, on they go,
Down the path that leads to woe,

*On reading in the Zion's Herald, a request for recollections
of the early ministers.*

LORENZO DOW.

I cannot tell you if I would,
All their exploits by field and flood,
But I may venture to rehearse
All that I know, in simple verse.
And well do I remember now,
That good old saint, Lorenzo Dow ;
What ere we call him, saint or sage,
He was the marvel of the age.

O, how can I depict his face,
Or try his lineaments to trace,
Since I must draw from memorys store,
To say the least, of years three score.
And yet it seems to me to-day,
As if it were but yesterday,
And I may venture to define,
The picture found within my mind.

A man with wondrous power possessed,
One the master owned and blessed,
If I might venture so to speak,
He was both tragic and unique.

7

His hair and beard so long and straight,
Extended downward to the waist,
His wrinkled face that frowned e're while,
Was seldom lighted by a smile.

As o'er the pulpit bending low,
His arms extending too and fro,
His finger pointing, and fixed eye,
Seemed the plague-spot to descry ;
And made the sinner shrink within,
As he portrayed their secret sin,
And one poor soul was in such a lurch,
That he quickly rose and left the church.

And when as a victim of God's wrath,
The fire and flame before him passed,
'Neath the stormy gust of passions swell,
O, then he was invincible !
With an emphatic beck and nod,
He conjured up the man of God,
Who in his wandering over night,
Took lodgings with the Shunammite.

And she, his wishes to forestall,
Built him a chamber in the wall,
And furnished it as she was able.
With a bed, a candlestick and table.
And he the type of the holy one
Foretold the coming of a son,

According to the sacred page,
To be the comfort of her age.

And she, unwilling to believe,
Fearing the prophet might deceive,
Yet when the time foretold had come,
She found in her embrace a son.
And all at once and all too soon,
The bud had withered ere high noon,
For being led by childish sport
Among the reapers to resort.

He, rushing to his father said,
Crying aloud, "my head, my head,"
His father sent him from the field,
His illness did to nothing yield.
With a fond mother's sympathy,
She tended him upon her knee ;
And in his intervals of pain
Would press him to her heart again.

And ne'er her eye from off him took,
And yet received no answering look ;
And though her heart might well have quailed,
Her faith and courage never failed.
And when her soft endearments press,
Received no answering caress,
And his closed lips to her revealed
That unto her his lips were sealed,

She saw her remedies had failed
And nothing had her care availed,
And as by inspiration led
She laid him on the prophet's bed.
For she who had his blessing shared,
And so carefully his room prepared,
Now felt that if it could be done,
The prophet would restore her son.

And to her husband straightway said,
"Saddle the ass, our child is dead."
"But wherefore go away so soon?
'Tis not the Sabbath or high noon."
"Nay tarry not, for it must be so
That to the prophet I must go."
Her husband hastened to obey
And sent a servant by the way.

Her accents on his ear that fell
Were—"forward drive, it shall be well;"
And forth she went as it was meet,
That she the prophet might entreat.
She might have breathed among the hills
Airs that had kissed a thousand rills,
Or have inhaled the healing balm
That nestled in their groves of palm.

Crushing beneath her hasty tread,
The fragrant lily in its bed ;
But on she drove o'er hill and dell,
Ne'er halting till she reached Carmel.
And Elisha saw, being keen of sight,
The coming of the Shunammite,
He, seeing her so much perplexed,
Thought something must her soul have vexed.

Pointing to his servant Gehazi,
He said unto the woman "hie ;"
The point on which Dow loved to dwell
Was this one's answer, "It is well."
"Well, with the husband and the child
It is well" she said in accents mild.
And, bending forward, she inclined
To reverence as to the divine.

But Gehazi could not refrain
This simple homage to restrain ;
Hinder her not ; my God forbid,
For he this thing from me hath hid.
Then by a kindly impulse led,
He sent his servant on ahead,
Reaching forth Gehazi his staff,
Saying "greet no one as you pass."

Roused by the tone in which he spoke,
The mother's heart in her awoke,
Nay as the Lord and my soul live,
Faith in no other can I receive.
Seeing her faith persistent still,
He arose and followed at her will,
For now, alas! he must be there,
To offer heaven such fervent prayer.

He knew in vain was staff or rod,
The breath of life must come from God,
And filled with this divine intent,
Up to his room the prophet went.
And by a special gift of grace
He threw himself on the young child's face,
And breathed upon the lifeless clay,
Taking himself by turns away.

Then bending o'er the cold, still form,
He felt the life-blood pulsing warm,
And that which had been dead before.
The hue of life and feeling wore.
And with a faith that death disarms,
It seemed but to renew his charms;
And pacing backward too and fro,
He said unto the woman "go."

When she into his presence ran,
He said to her "take up thy son."
Knowing in whom she had believed,
She thought no more of being deceived.
But in an ecstasy so sweet,
She fell in raptures at his feet,
Ere clasping his dear form around,
She bowed herself unto the ground.

Of her no more is said about,
But that she took him, and went out,
We see she drank life's bitter cup,
And had the faith that held her up.
And of her sufferings who can tell,
Since she affirmed " it was all well,
It is all well" she said, for so it must,
But it was all through faith and trust.

Oh how can I describe the spell
That like magic on the audience fell,
And midst gestures wild, and beck, and nod,
We felt he was the man of God.
Now lifting us above our fears,
And then dissolving us in tears.
Enough that he portrayed a faith
That will sustain us until death.

THE SEWING GIRL.

I am weary, weary of the world,
　With all its care and strife,
I am weary of the aching toil,
　That's wearing out my life.
For from the very earliest dawn
　Of daylight, to its close,
I have nought to do but sit and sew,
　And ponder o'er my woes.

Vainly have I combated my hopes
　With doubts and fears,
The shadows of a life time,
　Are closing round my years ;
If with an equal courage,
　I look them in the face,
The moment I have conquered one,
　Another takes its place ;
For dark misfortunes sable train,
　Attend where'er I go,
The phantoms thicken on my brain,
　And shape the coming woe.

When midst dark vicissitudes,
　We see the hand of God,
How patiently can we submit,
　And humbly kiss the rod ;

Yet there may be an added cup
  To this our Father sends :
The coldness and ingratitude,
  And treachery of friends.

This opens an unsightly wound,
  And deeper yet the stings,
In that it sends no soothing balm,
  No healing in its wings ;
Yet even from this may faith look up
  To brighter worlds above,
And revel in the glorious hope,
  Of God's abounding love.

TO A YOUNG STUDENT.

Just merging from thy boyhood, free from all care
  and strife,
Upon the threshold standing of a young and vigorous life ;
Look calmly on the brilliant hopes that gild the
  coming years,

S

Imploring heaven's assistance in dispersing cares
and fears.
Upon the stormy sea of life thou shalt embark ere
long,
Stemming with bold and fearless heart a current
deep and strong.
Swift sailing o'er the swelling flood, securely if
thou will,
Enough of danger lurks beneath for a ready pilot's
skill.
Deep hidden neath those sparry caves, far from all
human eye,
Growing within their coral beds the gems of ocean
lie.
Would'st have a treasure richer far than gold, or
gems ere bought?
It lies in grandeur of the soul; in majesty of
thought.
Conception of the beautiful a higher joy impart ;
Kindles a rapture in the soul, and elevates the
heart.
How skilful should'st thou steer thy bark o'er this
tempestuous sea,
Oft seeking wisdom from a source superior to thee.
Or diving neath the sparkling wave bring out the
pearls of thought,
Deep hidden 'neath the surface there, nor found if
never sought.

ACROSTIC.

How thy pure soul to deeds of mercy glow!
Each high resolve is written on thy brow.
Revered by all who chance to know thy worth,
Moving among the gayer scenes of earth.
In thee indeed a model may be found,
Of all the virtues clustering round.
'Neath all the charm of intellect I trace,
Enhanced by simple elegance and grace.
Honored in all the varied walks of life,
Of mother, daughter, sister, friend or wife.
O, may no cloud of sadness lingering near,
Disturb the evening of thy blissful year.

LIFE.

O glorious thought. with wonder strife,
The earth teems with a hidden life,
And wheresoe'er we glance the eye,
What infinite variety.

Stretch thought into its utmost range,
Nothing is lost though all be changed,
All living things, all times, each place
Bear marks of change upon its face.

Ask the philosopher and sage,
The wit and wisdom of the age,
To explain the hidden mystery,
How out of chaos all could be.

To be by that one little word,
The fountains of the soul are stirred;
To feel a life within so fraught.
With power of action and of thought.

From our existence first we claim,
A being without end or aim ;
Our first instinct, a sorrowing wail
For all the wants that life entail.

Dependent helplessness at best,
Unconscious that it is so blest,
With sense and intellect refined,
The God-like attributes of mind.

THE YOUNG BRIDE.

So young and lovely, with thy fond, true heart,
Thou hast been called thus early to depart.
With gentle patience thou didst smile on pain,
While love and hope wooed thee to life again.
Ye who watched her sadly day by day,
Knew every symptom of her slow decay ;
Ye saw the hectic fever's mantling glow.
The sure precursor of the insidious foe.

Ah, vain the patient skill so true and kind !
Even mighty love her spirit could not bind.
And when you gently hinted of your fears,
It but unsealed the fountain of her tears.
Then o'er her face a holy calmness stole,
And fortitude again possessed her soul.
And when she heard the summons of her God
She meekly bowed and passed beneath the rod.

At that hushed hour—the holy sabbath morn,
When song of bird on softest breeze is borne,
Just as the eastern sky was tinged with light,
Her angel spirit took its heavenward flight.
'Tis scarce two summers since her bridal day,
And scarcely has she lain her robes away,
Ere amid summer flowers, and song and bloom,
Another bridal waits her in the tomb.

Oh! marvel not that in the tomb she's laid.
The fairest flowers are those that soonest fade.
So transient is their beauty and their bloom,
They wither ere they scarce have reached their noon.
Why should you shed o'er her the bitter tear,
Since she has joined a higher, holier sphere?
And if her earthly ties have here been riven,   •
O, how much purer is the bliss of heaven!

THE EMPRESS CATHERINE.

Proud Empress of a mighty race,
Caring not whom she might debase;
She only felt that from her grasp
Some portion of her power had passed.

For a change had come.   Fate threatened
To snatch the Diadem from her brow;
And what would be her queenly dower
Of golden gems, if robbed of power?

And now behold her going forth,
Glittering with gems of priceless worth.
On the round and polished arm alone,
The light of glittering diamonds shone.

And lent their brilliance to a face
Of matchless and surpassing grace,
Whose witching elegance combined
To dazzle the beholder's mind.

In stately grandeur on she went,
Unto the vizier's royal tent.
With suppliant air, and look so sweet,
She laid her jewels at his feet.

And he, bewildered by the blaze
And fascination of her gaze,
And pleased perhaps with such a task,
Gave all that she presumed to ask.

And now of all her power possessed,
Does no sad thought disturb her breast,
That she some day may come to rue
The mercy she has pleased to sue.

For with her power once more regained,
Tighter she draws her victim's chains,
What if just heaven avenge the deed
That caused so many hearts to bleed !

FAREWELLS.

How vain, alas! were words to tell
The anguish of that last farewell.
It was bliss to feel that thou wert nigh,
And pain to hear the parting sigh.

How oft at dewy eve we strayed
Down to some lovely woodland shade :
Or, lingering near some grassy dell,
Gathered the flowers we loved so well ;

Or striving, as we strolled the beach,
Its hidden mysteries to reach ;
Or listening to the sea-shells roar,
We sought to know its mystic lore.

It were better far to understand
Him who wrote upon the sand ;
And turn our glance unto that shore,
Where such sad partings are no more.

IMPROVEMENTS OF THE AGE.

Not now as when Pegasus soared,
    With a rider on his back;
Upon his winged pathway
    He left no shining track.
Great truths in their development.
    May not be clearly seen;
But by their shining footprints,
    We know where they have been.

As thought, on her elastic spring,
    Goes on from stage to stage,
How slowly does she garner up
    The wisdom of the age.
For with her wild ambitions,
    And speculative dreams,
The present is the summing up
    Of what the past hath been.

And self-sufficient as she seems,
    While hurrying on so fast,
She pours into her ample lap,
    The gleanings of the past.
For now, as in the ages past,
    We hear it said of some—
If thought is written on the brow,
    " We see a dreamer come."

9

In his research for hidden truths,
　He leaves the written page,
Advances from well-travelled ground,
　Into the coming age.
Now seizing at the slightest clue,
　Which science's aid imparts,
He compasses with steady view,
　The end for which he starts.

He even doubts realities,
　And does not seem content
Until he yields, as if compelled,
　A wondering assent.
And when the world has ceased to doubt,
　And all their fears have fled,
Acknowledge the simplicity
　That to such wonders led.

He steals away from men awhile
　In quiet haunts to rove,
And listen to the wooing voice,
　Of nature in her grove.
In sounds, like many voices,
　Come answers to his soul,
An utterance responsive,
　To the harmonious whole.

He reads the music of the spheres,
    Their range however far,
Together with the name and use
    And distance of each star.
Pale watchers when the curtained night,
    Droppeth her mantel o'er,
Ye sentinel, the entrance port
    To the eternal shore.

The splendor of whose radiance
    With glory floods the soul,
So harmonize the beauty
    And order of the whole.
As with a prophet's ready ken,
    He reads their mystic lore,
His very soul is stirred within
    By seeing things before.

He gathers wisdom from the stones,
    By giving them a face ;
And simple types of the Divine,
    Are all the human race.
He sees the All-creative Power
    In the minutest things,
And draws his inspiration
    From these fresh and living springs.

He looks into the minds of men,
  And their designs can trace ;
And seeing their capacity,
  Assigns to each his place.
Giving to many-sided themes
  A meaning, simply true,
And clothes the old and hacknied thought
  With drapery anew.

The spirit of research demands
  A large and wider scope,
And all the treasures of the earth
  Their hidden sources ope,
The flood-gates of industrial life
  Pour forth a steady stream,
While many streets and thoroughfares
  Hiss forth the power of steam.

The monster does not puff in vain ;
  But in his power is worth ;
He boldly threatens, in his rage
  To girdle all the earth.
The vast resources of the time
  Keep on their steady pace,
And thus we see the elements
  Are harnessed in the race.

Since intellect and nature now
  Are joined by wedlock's band,
The offspring of their teeming brain,
  Come readily to hand.
While genie of the earth and air,
  Their magic influence lend,
And e'en the flashing fires of heaven,
  Their aid to genius lend.

For swift as even winged thought,
  Or magic of wild fire,
Annihilating time and space,
  Words fly along the wire.
For scarcely is the embryo thought
  Conceived within the brain,
Ere with this lightning speed tis caught,
  And echoed round the main.

While art and science do their best
  To elevate the mind,
Immense establishments arise
  To benefit mankind.
Here thousands toil from morn till night,
  Their fellow-men to bless,
And patient industry is crowned
  With something like success.

Learning content from their employ
They have no more to dread,
For virtue finds its own reward
And haunting fears have fled.

Brooding o'er all, an angel flings
The shadow of his broad-cast wings.
Help us to magnify thy power,
Presiding genius of the hour,
Embodiment of truth and grace.
Guarding illimitable space,
Infinity of atoms fast
Centre of the eternal past.

THE LITTLE BIRD.

A little bird shoots forth
With lightning speed,
Bearing within his mouth
The tiniest of seed.

He wings his upward flight,
  O'er mount, and stream and tree,
To summer's far off climes.
  Or islands of the sea.

The little seed has dropped
  Upon a fertile soil ;
Springs up without the aid
  Of culture or of toil.
The germ of life puts forth,
  In numerous little shoots,
Extending far and wide,
  Its many fibrous roots.

A foothold readily gained,
  It springs aloft and stands
A glorious, wide-spread tree,
  Magnificently grand.
Its lopping branches have
  · A fine protection made ;
And the tenderest of vows
  Are plighted 'neath its shade.

And in a few more years
  Where the very first arose,
Has sprung up into life,
  A beauteous sylvan grove.

That little bird upon the wing
  Scattering the seed behind,
Has raised a charming, leafy grove,
  For hundreds of its kind.

SUMMER RAMBLES.

I.

Ah! well do I remember
  The paths we wandered o'er;
Down through a green and tangled wood
  That led us to the shore.

And many a little flowery nook
  We turned aside to greet,
And rest our weary limbs awhile
  Upon a grassy seat.

Sometimes we sauntered 'mong the pines,
  And traced the little rills,
That with a gentle, murmuring sound
  Came running down the hills.

And when we reached the fragrant grove,
  We listened to the winds,
That with their own sweet melody
  Came sighing through the pines.

And never was the air perfumed
  With odor half so sweet,
As from this carpet that we trod,
  Of flowers 'neath our feet.

We loitered on the shady banks,
  Till hearts were well attune
With every wild, sweet melody,
  And glowing life of June.

Then up again and off to seek
  The shady vine-clad bowers,
Where, in such rich abundance,
  Grew the lovely wildwood flowers.

And down the deepest valleys
  Half-hid from human view,
The mayflowers and the violets
  Luxuriantly grew.

II.

Again have I revisited
  The dear, remembered spot,
Enhanced by recollections
  Which can never be forgot.

10

All nature wore the same glad look
  Of gay and smiling ease,
And the holly, for a brighter shade,
  Had changed her soft, green leaves.

The flowering locust still sent forth
  Its fragrance on the air,
And mingled with the song of life
  Resounding everywhere.

And at the silent hush of eve,
  When song of bird was done,
Old ocean took the anthem up,
  And kept it sounding on.

For, since the first sweet bridal morn
  Was ushered in by time,
Those surging billows have rolled on
  To the music of their chime.

Dashing majestically along,
  With white foam beaded o'er,
Or, hushed to an unquiet rest,
  Rippling along the shore.

The sunshine dancing on the wave,
  Flashed out a golden light,
Reflecting in its thousand rays,
  A wealth of diamonds bright.

But lovelier when the calm, pale moon
  A slivery flood outpours
On the wavy crest, the ocean's breast.
  To the dipping of the oars.

O, if there is a rest for us,
  When heaven to earth comes down,
'Tis when the soul in harmony
  With such loved scenes is found.

We feel the Omnipresent
  His seal on all has set,
And tuned our hearts to melody
  With all that we have met.

THE SILENT GUEST.

In ancient times a traveler
  Returning from the East,
Among the nobles of the land,
  Was bidden to a feast.

A gay and numerous company
   In gorgeous robes were dressed,
And every succeeding one
   Seemed gayer than the rest.

And there, while wit and mirth went round,
   And music filled the room,
The very air seemed laden
   With the costliest perfume.
The table groaned beneath the weight
   Of that delicious clime ;
While sparkled forth from jeweled cups,
   The rich, red, glowing wine.

But there was one among the throng
   Sat silent, stern and pale,
A flowery garland wreathed his brow,
   And over all a veil.
And of the richest viands there,
   He deigned not to partake,
But still reclining at the board,
   He neither laughed nor spake.

A feeling of mysterious awe
   Crept o'er the wondering guest,
Prompting the strange inquiry
   He dared not to express.

And turned he from the merry group,
　　All joyous as they seemed,
To gaze upon the silent form,
　　Of sad and solemn mein.

The feast was ended, and the guests
　　Departed, all save one ;
Still fixed and motionless he sat,
　　Dejected and alone.
That shrouded form had still retained
　　Its dignified repose,
Its same unchanging attitude,
　　Up to the banquet's close.

The ardent Greek with stealthy step,
　　Fearing his strength might fail,
Returned unto the banquet hall,
　　And threw aside the veil.
And lo! beneath those splendid robes,
　　And flowers so fresh and fair,
A dim, unsightly skeleton
　　Had been concealed with care.

It was an eloquent device
　　Of men renowned and high.
To teach them in their hours of mirth.
　　That death is ever nigh.

The certain, yet uncertain end
　　Of mortal joy and care ;
The end of all their hopes and fears,
　　For this they must prepare.

For though the worn and weary soul
　　That longs to be at rest.
Is sometimes called to wing its way
　　To the mansions of the blest.
Yet full as oft the joyous soul
　　That fain would longer stay,
In the dewey morning of its youth
　　Is soonest called away.

PROGRESS.

Ever keep open to thy view
　　The point that thou wouldst gain ;
Some bright ideal of the soul,
　　To which thou must attain.

What if at first the summit,
 Should cloud-capped seem to be ;
Look onward to the opening,
 The golden tops thou'lt see.

Nay, murmur not, nor falter ;
 Why think it all in vain,
If thou shouldst fall far shorter
 Than is thy highest aim ?

The conflict may be sharpened
 By toil and pains and care,
And lurking evils all unseen
 May prove to thee a snare.

'Tis not by hurrying madly on,
 Like rash, expectant youth,
That thou may'st ever hope to reach
 The higher plains of truth.

If groping darkly in the maze
 Of error or of doubt,
Let faith point to the glimmering star,
 If faintly it shines out.

Say :—if each hidden moment
 The future brings to light,
Shall it bear a blotted record,
 Or shall the page be white ?

The present may be witness
  To thy firm and high resolve,
Thus steadily advancing,
  Life's problems thou may'st solve.

O, would thou be persuaded?
  It is no empty sound;
The soul that once has struggled
  Can ne'er be losing ground.

By seeking, cometh knowledge;
  And after toil, comes rest;
And only thus by striving,
  Can the true soul be blest.

Yet, earnest soul, look onward,
  O'er the mental strife.
List to the silent prompting
  Of thy true, inner life.

Uncertain is thy progress,
  Whate'er may be thy needs,
Unless the record of each day,
  Bear witness to thy deeds.

Why dost thou waste in doing
  That which may ne'er be done;
If idly thus pursuing
  Life's great momentous sum?

By trifling at the onset,
  And turning from the race,
Sure ne'er was feat accomplished
  By such uncertain pace.

For he who trod the wine-press,
  Has onward gone before,
And opened up a pathway
  To the eternal shore.

And those who reach the portal
  Must pass beneath the rod,
Ere they receive admission
  To the paradise of God.

PARSON PECK'S BABY.

Our pastor's folks had scarcely settled down,
When a new baby came to town :
The sickly wife was getting worse,
So mother took the babe to nurse.

11

He was a wee, small little speck,
Although his name was Baby Peck ;
The measure was indeed quite short,
He scarce would fill a common quart.
We take to gems and curious fossils,
And any dainty little morsels,
And so it came, as time went round,
The child a good, kind home had found.
The mother, on life's downward road,
Was lightened of one-half her load ;
But we could scarce repress a frown
At baby's dark blue cotton gown,
Worn o'er a yellow flannel skirt,
Made to seem innocent of dirt.
We were not rich, but none the less
Did we dislike that funny dress.
As it sometimes happens among the poor,
Of baby clothes we'd quite a store ;
And so of course the little mite,
On company days appeared in white.
In after years it was well known
That baby was to a bishop grown.
We scarcely could conceal our joy
When thinking of that little boy.
This simple tale the lesson brings
To ne'er despise the smallest things.

FOREST VOICES.

Through the towering cedars
  And dark pine trees,
List! hear the soft murmur,
  And catch the fresh breeze,
As their many-toned voices
  Sweep over the soul ;
O, hushed are its murmurs,
  And sweet its control.

For nature speaks to sorrowing minds,
  In strange, weird tones,
Through the whispering pines.
  With their low moans ;
Conveying in language
  Solemn and new,
Rich lessons of wisdom,
  Earnest and true.

Yes ; nature's voices
  Are sweeter to none
Than the stricken heart,
  That is sorrowing alone.
Alone with its God,
  'Midst the deep stillness there,
Come the still, small voices,
  In answer to prayer.

THE WRECKERS.

The wreckers, as usual engaged in o'erturning
  Whatever belonged to their honest employ,
Were startled at what on more closely discerning,
  Had proved the remains of a beautiful boy.
      'Midst the billows roar,
      Tossed on the shore.

There was all the charm of childhood,
  In that beautiful, upturned face,
And the damp dews on his forehead,
  Could not rob it of its grace ;
      Tossed on the crest
      Of the ocean's breast.

Where were his father and mother
  Whose christian name he bore ?
Where were the sister and brother ?
  Had they all gone on before?
      Did the cruel wave
      Their limp forms lave ?

There was no sign of the trouble
  Or anguish, that they could trace,
Of his wild and fearful struggle
  In the cold, dark waves embrace.
      All alone
      With the sad sea's moan.

The naiads gathered around him
  'And his slumbering eyelids pressed,
O'er the lustrous orbs forever dim ;
  And the seal on his lips had set,
      No more to wake
      Till the morning break.

The damp seaweed his cold limbs dressed.
  And wrapped him as in a shroud,
And on the heaving billows breast,
  He was borne as in a cloud,
      To the spirits' home,
      No more to roam.

SPRING.

The very thought of thee, O spring
A joy unto the soul dost bring ;
Thou breakest the icy monarchs chain.
And crystalled streams leap forth again.

Behold the thousand little rills
Come running over rocks and hills,
Their playful eddies seem to hush,
Then gather force and onward rush.

Rejoicing o'er their onward way,
They sparkle in the sun's bright ray,
While coursing downward to the sea,
With rippling murmurs we are free.

The winding stream with grasses twin'd.
And gold and emerald, interlined,
Glides on so noiseless all the day,
And gathers force along its way.

O genial sound with rapture heard
Of purling brook. and singing bird,
Of budding leaf, and flowering tree,
All, all are beautiful to see.

Each tiny bud that bursts the sod,
Unfolds to view a thought of God,
And as the little flowers expand,
They tell us of a Father's hand.

There's not a little flower or leaf,
Its fragile life however brief.
But ere it withers, and departs,
Conveys its lesson to our hearts.

THE PILGRIM FATHERS.

They stemmed the ocean's wrath
　With a spirit stern and brave,
And left no track on the ocean's path,
　But the foam of the surging wave.
They bade farewell to home,
　Its luxuries and ease,
And sought this wilderness alone,
　Their conscience to appease.

And when they reached the land,
　The rock on which we rest,
The first of all the pilgrim band
　By woman's foot was pressed.
Yes, foremost in the race
　Among that little band,
Came woman, with angelic grace,
　To lend a helping hand.

They caught a dim foretaste
　Of blessings to the free,
Before them stretched the wintry waste,
　And onward rolled the sea.
Firm and unmoved they stood,
　With souls serene and clear,
Their joy flowed forth in gratitude
　Exalted and sincere.

And foremost in the place,
  Soon as they reached the land,
They met a wild and dusky race,
  And took them by the hand.
With hearts devoid of fear,
  They ranged the hills and slopes,
And laid upon this alter here
  The offering of their hopes.

Oh, what a train of woes
  Beset that little band,
By treacherous, hostile foes,
  Beseiged on every hand ;
See now with patient toil
  Their faces heavenward set,
The coward soul with fears recoil
  From the dangers that they met.

Whence came their hardihood,
  No inch or jot to bate,
But the incoming of the good,
  The shaping hand of fate.
No cheerful cottage light,
  No ruddy fireside blaze,
Shone out upon the wintry night,
  To meet their longing gaze.

But the mighty axe descends,
  And the pliant saplings bow,
And the curling wreaths of smoke ascend
  Where camp-fires blazed e're now.
Before their patient toil,
  The redman must recede,
And their assumptions of the soil,
  Succumb to title deed.

They braved the tempest's wrath,
  And felled the ponderous trees,
And when they crossed the redman's path,
  His anger must appease.
A foe forever at hand,
  Nimble and swift of feet :
They, the possessors of the land,
  To whom revenge was sweet.

For sacred were the mounds,
  Above their fathers' bones,
And every forest tree around
  Had its familiar tones.
And now the dread war-whoop
  Is borne upon the breeze,
And dusky forms come skulking round
  Among the forest trees.

12

A dark and bloody strife,
  A contest hand to hand,
With tomahawk and scalping knife,
  The fire and smoking brand,
The course which they pursued,
  Must be ordained of heaven,
For all their sad vicissitudes
  Seemed but the gospel leaven.

To them the happiest day
  In all life's busy round,
Was when the Indian tramped away
  Off to his hunting ground.
Her forests and the woods
  With verdure overran,
And her primeval solitudes
  Waited the coming man.

As it must be with the weak
  When struggling for the wrong,
Their subjugation was complete,
  And victory with the strong.
They took their onward march,
  Where the Great Spirit led :
Through the dense woods triumphal arch,
  Bearing along their dead.

And many a cheek grew pale,
  At those unearthly tones,
That mingled with the forest wail
  And the low surges moans.
The dirge-like strain so wild and free
  With natures voices blent,
And the sounding caverns of the sea
  Echoed the wild lament,
As the warriors of a savage race
  With measured steps moved on,
Firm and erect a steady pace
  Toward the setting sun.

THE HUMAN WILL.

Say, who, if they should look about,
  Would honestly engage
In their own self to carry out
  The follies of the age.
For rank weeds find in such a soil
  Plenty of room to thrive ;
Hot beds without care or toil,
  Keep the roots alive.

Here first of all his office to fulfil,
Enthroned all powerful, is the human will.
Where in dread umpire sitting side by side,
Sybil and priest their oracles divide.
Clothed in the royal trappings of a state,
They wait upon and thus decide our fate ;
Seeking alike to judge and to preside,
Sole arbiter of both our loss and pride.

Kept in subjection, it will be most true :
But blindly yielding, it will conquer you.
Its slightest wish in clam'rous tones are heard,
And urging oft the hasty deed and word.
Say what you will, obtain what you will have,
Lord of creation, you are still the slave.
Its lightest mandates quick you must obey ;
It brooks no rival, suffers no delay ;

But hurries on its victim to his final doom,
As the fated vessel to the dread monsoon.
As may be seen, by such fierce passions led,
The rank rebellion reared its hydra head.
The north, convulsed, uttered the deepest groans,
While southern despots spoke in thunder tones.
A nation, roused amid its hopes and fears,
Rushed to a conflict ending not for years.

For tyranny, oppression, and for wrong,
The day of reckoning had surely come.
The sword of justice, flaming red,
Scourge-like, is hanging overhead.
A subtile essence all unseen is rife,
Pervading every avenue of life ;
Nearing the citadel, attacks each part,
Enters at once into its deepest heart.

Within the very shadow of their home,
The patriot martyrs in their dungeons groan,
Or water with their very blood, the soil
On which the slave has spent his life in toil.
Shame on the souls that listened to their moans!
Why were not voices given to the stones,
That they might cry the utterance of their shame—
Kindling men's hearts into a living flame?

Millions of sufferers feel that they have naught to
        lose,
So dark their fate, so heavy are their woes ;
Imploring heaven with heartfelt, earnest prayer,
They bide their time in calmness of despair.
Led by the immortal Grant, there fell stroke after
        stroke,
Until, by an o'erwhelming force, they broke the
        galling yoke.

Then a glad nation's voice rang out in shouts of
    victory,
And the martyred Lincoln's pen soon set the
    bondsmen free.

The nation raised for each a funeral pyre ;
While hilltops and the valleys gleamed with fire.
Like those rich draughts which kindly nature
    yields
In rich abundance, from her spicy fields,
Love welled from hearts, the lowliest and the great,
While praises rang from north to southern state.
How loud and joyous echoed heaven's high dome,
When their great souls by angels were borne
    home.

A SHIPWRECK.

As I strolled by the beach one beautiful morning,
    With its rosetinted shells and bright weeds
    strewn o'er,
Which the saucy wild waves so playfully scorning,
    Had carelessly thrown up in heaps on the shore.

Nowhere on the earth could a place be imagined
  More recklessly wild or luxuriantly free,
Where the trees of the forest all in concert united
  With the murmuring sounds of the dark, heav-
    ing sea.
We sat on the rocks and looked out on the ocean.
  At a little dark speck a few leagues from the
    shore,
Where an emigrant ship with her passengers laden:
  Had sunk on that rock just a few days before.
    With the wildbird's winged motion,
      Her homeward course did take,
    Leaving no track on the ocean,
      But the beaded foam in her wake.
    Their hearts bounding so lightly,
      With bliss quite brimming o'er,
    Sent up their offering nightly,
      As they neared the distant shore.
Full oft in fleeting visions their vagrant fancies
  roved,
  And clasped in dreams elysian the forms of their
    beloved.
The bounding ship came dashing onward ;
  She hailed the land and struck her lights,
And the blissful dreams that lured them forward,
  With fairy visions mocked their longing sight.

What fearful intimation roll on that heaving sea,
 As vast and boundless in its scope, as is eter-
  nity!
No shadowy future met their glancing;
 The winged hours seem draped in white,
And joyfully given to song and dancing—
 In mirthful pleasures they passed the night.
  There was gay, expectant youth.
   And age serene and mild,
  From the gentle girl with heart of truth,
   Down to the little child.
How wildly fearful dawned the morning,
 When lashed to fury in their wrath,
The fearful elements gave warning
 Of the storm king thundering on his path.
And now she stands aloft with a bearing wild and
 free,
 Then plunging down, seems wholly lost beneath
  the angry sea.
Wilder and wilder grew the storm;
 Swift and more swift she neared the shore;
And rude rocks reared their threatening forms,
 And billows dashed the proud ship o'er.
They see all hope is gone, for the mountain bil-
 lows roll,
And the fated ship is plunging on, freighted
 with human souls.

With a lightning speed she dashed upon that
    treacherous rock,
And her lower decks are parted by that first sud-
    den shock.
But a still more fearful crash, a wilder shriek of
    woe,
As the breakers o'er them dash and the cabins fill
    below.
    Once more, it is the last,
        An agonizing wail
    Has mingled with the angry blast,
        And flesh and spirit fail.
    For a home in the glad, new world,
        They had come o'er the bounding wave,
    And as they neared its threshold,
        They found a watery grave.
    For the yawning gulf opes wide,
        And their resting place must be
    Where mermaids fair their treasures hide
        In the chambers of the sea.

DEDICATION OF PINE GROVE CEMETERY.

And is that all, that little spot of earth,
Where lighter green grows the turf,
The gently raised, the grassy mound,
With taller monuments around ;

All that remains of that fair form
Glowing with rich affections warm,
Flushed with the joy of loves young dream,
As transient as a meteors gleam ?

Ah, yes, the truth upon us broke,
Upon the hillside's sunny slope
She sleeps, who late in all her pride,
Appeared so fresh a blooming bride.

I met her first where pine trees wave
In murmurs o'er the silent grave,
'Twas in a shady woodland grove,
A resting place for all who chose.

Where altogether now had come,
To consecrate their final home ;
The song of birds the flowers and trees
The rustling of the soft green leaves :—

All lent their influence to the hour,
Made sacred by the spirit's power;
Invoked by one whose voice and mien,
'Twixt man and heaven might come between.

For even his tone, his looks, his air,
All breathed the eloquence of prayer,
And from his lips such accents fell
Upon the ear and heart as well.

Glowing with faith and hope sublime,
Just suited to the place and time.
The heavenly import of his words
In strict accordance with our Lord's,
All hallowed ever by that sign,
Thy will be done on earth, not mine.

And here we have the final test,
He giveth his beloved rest;
Even then I think we had our fears
She ne'er would count her life by years,
But there are some in deeds they say,
Gain what they lose another way.

And glancing down life's flowery slope,
Love beckoned on with joy and hope,
And the angels fanned her with their wings,
And whispered bright and beautiful things.

With one glad bound she met, it seemed
Her all of life in that bright gleam :
Ah hapless fate, ah woe betide,
Earth's promise to a fair young bride.

For now her friends were wont to say,
Death had been cheated of its prey,
It must be so, for she meanwhile
Had gained her strength and wonted smile.

But surely we must know full well
The angel death alone can tell,
Not caring if we are ready quite,
It is his to aim the blow, and strike.
No matter whether late or soon
All sharers of the same great doom,
Parting the seen from the unseen,
A turbid river rolls between.

A golden bridge the river spans,
Together crossing they clasp hands;
He the beloved her own heart's pride,
Chosen from all the world beside.

As two glad streams together run
Have met and mingled into one,
And having once joined company
Can never separated be, though seeming
Lost in that dark sea,
Preserving their identity.

FANCY FLIGHTS.

Thy plaintive tones in their shadowy way
Like airy nothings seem melting away,
Ye have touched a chord, a tremulous tone,
That thrills with sadness deep and lone.

On balmy zephyrs floating past,
Ye awaken feelings too pure to last;
And the fairy visions fade from our grasp
Like flickering moonbeams on our path.

Or borne aloft at the hush of even,
Like incense offered up to heaven,
And thus they go, the dearly loved
And cherished, to their home above.

Swift as a thought or even a breath.
Is hurried past the mission of death,
The idol of some, the joy of the crowd,
Lies buried 'neath the coffined shroud;
The father of all in goodness and love
Has gathered them in to the home above.

In Memoriam, and other Poems.

IN MEMORIAM.

—

JAMES P. BOYCE.

—

After we had talked of our prospects,
   And of him so late removed,
The dear wife read from the Prophets,
   The themes he so much loved.
I listened with close attention
   To the grand and lofty strains,
Until they came to mention
   The Name above all names.

As she read of the scene so tragic,
   Of Him, the Life, the Way,
We were touched as if by magic,
   With the Prophet's simple lay.
We turned our gaze up yonder,
   Our hearts were all, aflame.
As we heard with joy and wonder
   Of his exceeding fame.

14

For we felt in the early dawning,
　　When the mists were cleared away,
She might meet him in the morning
　　Of a bright and glorious day.
And she saw that 'neath the shadow
　　Of his wings she might find rest,
And find her missing treasures
　　In the mansions of the blest.

How she must miss him, who can say?
　　Since words have ne'er expressed
The depths of sorrow, that find way
　　Within the human breast.
We miss him in our social life;
　　His hopeful words of cheer
Urging us onward in the strife
　　With good and evil here.

So large a share of wedded bliss
　　It was their lot to gain,
As few in such a world as this
　　May hope to e'er attain.
At fragrant morn or dewy eve,
　　When book or work was done,
She could such pleasant fancies weave
　　Of his returning home.

Seeing him reading in his chair,
  Or writing at his desk,
When he an essay would prepare
  With his accustomed zest.
Or to see him at the table there—
  Each in their proper place --
Preside with his familiar air
  Of dignity and grace.

At last there came a change to them
  In an intervening hour ;
A tender bud upon the stem,
  That blossomed into flower.
With the sweet instincts of the dove,
  As tender and as true,
Forth on her ministry of love,
  Into their arms she flew,

And nestled down into their hearts,
  Whose tender, brooding care
Must surely be the angel's part,
  Who watch the entrance there.
She scarce had reached the border land,
  Where youth and girlhood meet,
Ere she perceived life's golden sands
  Were slipping 'neath her feet.

She has taken her upward flight,
  On through death's portal,
To bloom in realms of light,
  A flower immortal.
Smarting beneath the shock,
  How the frail hearts languish !
Clinging unto the Rock
  Must heal such anguish.

Submitting to his will,
  While passing 'neath the rod,
They heard the voice, " Be still
  And know that I am God ;"
As through the clouds of mists
  That sometimes intervene,
Through blinding gusts and parting rifts,
  The sunshine may be seen.

Where in the haunts of sin and vice,
  The dangers multiplied,
He must raise the warning voice,
  Or ne'er be satisfied.
And with clear perception
  Of the master's work in view,
He saw as in a vision
  God's sunlight shining through.

That he walked by faith and not by sight,
  It was evident to see ;
His witness of the inner light, was
  The truth had made him free.
He was among the first to reach
  The oppressed a helping hand ;
His energies of thought and speech
  Went broadcast o'er the land.

Rousing the dormant mind,
  Until the final stroke,
When the united nation joined
  To break the oppressor's yoke,
Intemperance in him
  Had an inveterate foe,
And he exhausted all his vim
  To lay the monster low.

Out from the wilderness of sin,
  His efforts were untold,
The weak and wandering to win
  To the good Shepherd's fold.
And they must be persuaded
  Of his earnestness and zeal,
Who were thus privileged
  To hear his eloquent appeal.

His gentle, calm benificence
   Shows in a clearer ray,
In deeds of pure benevolence
   Gilding life's dim pathway.
It was a fresh and living spring,
   Whose waters still and clear,
Quickened to life the hidden things,
   The sweet buds growing near.

While life still held for him a charm,
   Obedient to His will,
He leaned on the Almighty Arm,
   Calm, resolute and still.
And if his steadfastness be proved,
   Or faith put to the test,
He would, like him, the best Beloved,
   Have leaned upon his breast.

He seemed upon the wings of faith
   Triumphantly to ride,
And said that the celestial gate
   To him had opened wide.
Up in his Father's blest abode,
   Unspeakably bright,
He should appear in pure, white robes,
   And spotless, in His sight.

MY FATHER.

I think there must be on the whole,
  A lack of saving grace,
When in the poet's genial soul,
  His Father finds no place.
Musing upon the strange event,
  In the soft firelight's glow,
A hearing to my ear was lent,
  Of some one breathing low.
Away the phantom seemed to roll,
  From my bewildered sight:
While sweetly o'er my senses stole
  A vision of delight.
It may have been a transient gleam
  From out the firelight shine,
I was so sure that eyes that beamed,
  Were looking into mine.
The spirit I so longed to meet
  Was readily defined;
A form so perfect and complete,
  It seemed almost divine.
O, had the disembodied soul
  Come back to visit me?
I shouted, lost beyond control,
  "My father ! it is he !"

The softened outlines of a face
　Of one so true and kind,
That nothing ever could efface
　The impress from my mind.
In his dear lineaments to trace
　Our venerable head:
In the sweet expression of a face
　That for forbearance plead.
He had the principle within,
　Which to the souls belong,
Of whom it always may be said
　They would do nothing wrong.
And wheresoe'er his footsteps led
　Whether by field or flood,
It must be with the same intent,
　Of doing someone good.
And with such reverence profound,
　He read the sacred page
With grandchildren gathered round,
　The crown of his old age.
The racket of this little band,
　So frolicsome and bright,
Were ever to this aged pair
　A source of great delight.
They had their joys and sorrows,
　Yet ever on the way,

The promise of the morrow
  Was realized to-day.
They did not lose their happiness
  As they in turn grew old.
They realized a blessedness
  Repaying them tenfold.
Hope glided evermore
  Their darker hours between,
And vanished joys lived fondly o'er,
  Still kept the memory green.
At length the heaving sigh
  Gave token as it ought,
With the uplifting of the eye,
  That God was in their thought.
It was he who girded them at length;
  He was their staff and stay,
And he who led them by his strength
  Upon the shining way.
And they must be well satisfied
  When thro' His dear name's sake,
With loved among the glorified
  In his likeness they awake.

MY BROTHER.

Beloved, where art thou, whither fled ?
Since thou wert taken from thy lowly bed,
Where with an aspect of exceeding peace,
Thy soul in patience waited its release,
Amidst the silence and the gloom,
An unseen presence filled the room.
A solemn awe upon our spirits fell,
Knowing "He doeth all things well."
For by his chill and icy breath
We knew this messenger was death,
Whose hoary locks and solemn mein
Ourselves and loved ones came between.
And loosed the fetters that wrapped him round,
In a clay tenement, like prisoner bound;
In durance held, till on some fairer day
In all completeness thou should soar away.
With the wrapped host, say, dost thou soar and
            sing ?
In all this beauty hast thou seen the king ?
In fields elysian does thy spirit roam,
And in the many mansions find a home?
For aught we know swift messenger of love,
Among the innumerable courts above.
Of wisdom fathoming the height and length,
Ere going on from strength to strength;

Or, take a wider range from sun to sun,
In endless cycles ever, ever on;
Or, swiftly borne aloft on Angel's wing,
Up where the stars forever sing;
Or does thy soul in silent rapture wait
With souls redeemed at the golden gate?
Or far beyond the ken of human scope,
Do founts of knowledge to thy vision ope?
Or higher yet, to mortals ne'er allowed,
Float on the amber curtains of a cloud?
Back to thy Father's bosom didst thou fly,
Ecstatic glory seeking eye to eye?
No longer darkly now, but face to face,
With ransomed ones from every clime and place;
The white robed throng who all with one accord
In adoration bow before their Lord;
Or grasp the meaning of that sacred word,
"Eye hath not seen and ear hath never heard."
The joys sublime, unspeakably great,
Only reserved for those who watch and wait.
In vain I sound the fathomless abyss;
From that dread bourne, no answer comes to this.
Vainly our hopes take council of our fears,
And seek relief in sighs and moans and tears.
He opes to those the mysteries of grace,
In storm and calm, who see a father's face.
The darkest night to him is perfect day;
Before the light the darkness flees away.

YOUNG MOTHER.

Mother with chastened brow, thoughtful and mild,
Why gaze so earnest on thy darling child,
This tender bud to thy fond wishes given
It seems to be a precious gift from Heaven.

This tiny bud entrusted to thy care
Is wondrous bright and oh how passing fair,
So fairy like and full of witching wiles
Its little face all dimpled o'er with smiles.

How beautiful it looks as there it lies,
The love light slumbering in its dewy eyes,
While on its sunny brow so pure and fair,
Lie clustering ringlets of its golden hair.

Thy yearning heart mayhap seeks to divine
The bright immortal spirit there enshrined,
Who, all unconscious of thy mother's part,
Is twined so lovingly around thy heart.

Thou seekest methinks to read the hidden page
Which ne'er has been revealed to saint or sage,
What is its future promise, what may be
The unfolding of its higher destiny.

MY SISTER.

"I am going ; I am going,"
  My sister said one day,
"I feel that I must leave you,
  For I can no longer stay.
I have heard a voice you cannot hear,"
  She still went on to say,
"And see a hand you cannot see
  Which beckons me away."
The silver cord might loosened be ;
  And we could only pray
That He who rules the wind and wave,
  The tempest might allay :
And on the weak and stricken heart,
  The hand of healing lay.
"I cannot bear to leave you,
  And fain my grief would hide,
But I see my loved ones waiting
  For me on the other side."
O, could we but encourage her
  To bury the dead past,
And look onward to the future
  That seemed within her grasp !
She but needed a suggestion
  Of any kind or sort,
To strengthen her endeavor
  For any Christian work.

Day in and out hereafter
　　We saw her growing slim,
And while we sought to flatter,
　　Our hopes grew very dim.
Her nerves, like an Aeolian harp,
　　Seemed all too finely strung
For the sorrow and the anguish
　　With which her heart was wrung,
At the very thought of parting
　　With her dearest, best loved one,
"I never could outlive them !
　　I fear I should go wild !
I never could be parted
　　From my husband, and my child !"
And, yielding to a burst of grief,
　　Her voice would often fail,—
"But I see my loved ones waiting
　　Just beyond the vale."
Then, gathering comfort, she would speak
　　Of those she'd tried to bless,
And for her children sowed the seed,
　　Of truth and righteousness.
And as she spoke, her face
　　Was bright with glory in her soul ;
A glow so luminous and bright,
　　That o'er her features stole.

It long had been her chief delight
  Among the mighty throngs
To raise her voice in praise,
  To whom all praise belongs.
The inspiration of her soul
  Seemed welling from that fount
Which Moses' did at Pisgah's height,
  Upon the holy mount.
"I am going ; I am going."
  We feared she could not last;—
Alas ! we saw life's golden sands
  Were running down so fast!
And while we watched and soothed her,
  Still waiting by her side,
Her life went out so gently
  We knew not when she died.
Her voice on earth has ceased,
  But with the white-robed throng
We knew she'd e'er be singing.
  The sweet and grand "new song."

IN MEMORIAM.

Farewell, dear friend, farewell to life,
　Thy sufferings here are o'er,
Its haunting shadows, cares and strife,
　Can trouble thee no more.

Full of compassion to the last,
　For all, both far and near,
Not looking backward o'er the past,
　But onward, without fear.
Looking for wisdom from above,
　Ignoring sects or creeds ;
Giving her thought to works of love,
　And the sweet ministry of deeds.

Unmindful of herself at best
　If aught of suffering she knew,
Then forth upon her eager quest
　Instinctively she flew.

Vain were entreaties to arrest
　Her silent going forth,
For all who knew her, must attest,
　Her excellence and worth.
The lessons that experience brought,
　Were silently obeyed,
And never in her inmost thought,
　From their wise precepts strayed.

Her friendship was beyond this life ;
 Her love a tie that binds;
As mother, daughter, sister, wife,
 She left no one behind.
She yielded to the winsome grace
 Of childhood's tender years,
And the pattering of little feet
 Was music to her ears.

No tender bud of beauty rare
 E'er blossomed on that hearth,
But owed its fostering love and care
 To her who gave it birth.
With a patience more than mortal
 And a faith that was sublime,
She waited at the portal,
 To hear the heavenly chime.

And, as her list'ning ear
 Caught the angelic strain
Of seraph voices bright and clear,
 She joined the celestial train.

TO C. A. HAYDEN.

Come out from thy solitude,
  And fearless go forth,
As the eagle spreads out her
  Bright wings for the north.

So proudly careering
  O'er mountain and dome,
Thy genius untiring,
  Shall usher thee on.

Unfurl thy bright pinions
  To the favoring breeze :
Thy flight shall be onward,
  O'er oceans and seas.

How splendid and glorious
  Thy pathway appears ;
Triumphantly soaring
  O'er all thy compeers.

As upward and onward
  Thy spirit soars on,
What soul-stirring melody
  Floats in thy song!

In raptures, while soaring
　　The high heavens o'er,
Thy keen searching gaze,
　　Reads their deep, mystic lore.

Aye fix thy rapt gaze on that
　　Glorious abode,
That beautiful city,
　　The temple of God.

On, on, through deep azure,
　　Unceasingly on,
Allured by the brightness,
　　So dazzling it shone.

Thou mayst bask in the light
　　Of an undying fame ;
Unscorched by its radiance
　　Thou firm shalt remain.

Till thy spirit disrobed,
　　And transported above,
Shall bathe in a fount
　　Of ineffable love.

TO A YOUNG FRIEND.

He calleth thee to pastures fair,
By the still waters, calm and clear,
And through the mists that intervene,
His hand of leading may be seen.
 He leadeth thee, He leadeth thee ;
 By His own hand, He leadeth thee.

He to the earnest soul doth say—
" See that ye faint not by the way ;
Go slake your thirst from that supply
Of living springs that never dry.
 He leadeth thee, He leadeth thee ;
 By His own hand, He leadeth thee.

And to the hungry soul hath said,
" I'll feed thee with the living bread;"
It gives a power of self-control
That strengthens and restores the soul.
 He leadeth thee, He leadeth thee ;
 By His own hand, He leadeth thee.

It is thy privilege most sweet
To lay thy burdens at His feet,
Of whom it truly hath been said,
" No waiting soul need be afraid."
 And faint and weary tho' thou be,
 He leadeth thee, He leadeth thee.

CLARA.

She slept within a darkened room
Wrapt in the drapery of the tomb :
And slowly gathering one by one,
Mourners and friends together come.

They gazed upon the marble brow,
Where death has set its signet now.
The look she wore was sweet and mild ;
Her lips seemed parted in a smile.

Her form was pulseless, cold and chill ;
And yet the gazer felt no thrill,
Such was the sweetness and the grace
That rested on the calm, pale face.

It spoke of gentleness and love,
And peace that cometh from above,
And of a pure and holy faith,
That giveth victory over death.

For she had caught the heavenly gleam
Of light that o'er her vision beamed,
Bright and effulgent as the ray
That heralds in the new-born day.

They wiped the death-dew from her brow
Where resteth such a halo now ;
For when her spirit caught the ray,
It left its impress on the clay.

WALDO BRADLEY RUSSELL.

Why is it, in this active life of sorrow and of woe,
The loved and dearly cherished are oft the first to
    go?
That the very soul of honor with its high and holy
    trust,
The crown of early manhood, should be buried in
    the dust.

One whose highest aspirations, such a halo o'er him
    shed,
As seldom clusters round the name when one is
    with the dead.
That must have been a fruitful soil, and seasoned
    well with prayer,
So to repay the tillers' toil, and reap a harvest
    there.

As 'neath the vernal blessings of a shower,
Fruit-laden branches blossom forth in flower,
So his pure life, thus early snatched so soon,
Blossomed to fruitage ere manhood's noon.

His fortitude increased by suffering long ;
In faith's assurance growing yet more strong ;
Untiring in devotedness and zeal ;
His death, a loss which all must deeply feel.

How much more to her who was his brightest, best,
The sweet companion of his hours of rest,
The chosen one, with whom she hoped to glide
On through life's journey, gladly, side by side.

And such the promise in that blissful state,
It would seem on earth a happiness too great.
Her joy may be complete in that blest land ;
God knoweth best ; " Our times are in His hand."

How was that stricken mother's heart opprest,
That pillowed him so fondly on her breast.
He, round whom bright hopes were clustering
        high,
With dreams of happiness ; why must he die !

And the fond father, who with her divided
The deep solicitude, the joy and·pride,
So largely shared in the kind, loving heart
Of the dear grandma, who must do her part;

Soothing his sufferings day by day,
And bidding him look to " The Life, the Way."
A loving son, a brother, kind and true,
Disclosing traits, equalled by very few.

How happily they saw him going forth,
So proudly conscious of his sterling worth ;
Those very traits, endearing him to them,
Would rank him high among the best of men.

He might have figured in the roll of fame,
And to posterity have left a name.
No longer suffering on his bed of pain,
The loss to you, for him is so much gain.

What greater blessedness could he desire,
Than hear the Master's summons " Come up high-
        er ?"
In vestments white, before the throne to bow,
And have the " New Name " written on his brow.

MY COUSIN.

How is it that thy hours glide
 So peacefully along?
Thou hast no sorrow in thy heart,
 No sadness in thy song.
Knowing so little of the world,
 Its trials, cares and woes,
Thou art resting in a holy calm,
 A beautiful repose.
Thine is the sweet and touching charm
 That seeks no aid of art;
A simple elegance and grace,
 So sure to win the heart.
Within thy soul lie hidden depths
 Of love and sympathy,
Like those rich pearls embedded
 'Neath the caverns in the sea.
With feelings kind and tender,
 As pure, and warmly bright,
As is the diamond glowing
 With ever varying light.

17

TO A POETESS.

Can aught we say or think of thee
  Proclaim thy matchless worth ?
Among the bright celestial throng
  Thy spirit claims its birth.
Redeemed from sin by that pure blood's
  Atoning sacrifice,
O, may thy spirit's offering
  Up to His throne arise :
Like incense on the altar poured,
  A pure and hallowed flame,
Its deep-toned music gushing forth
  In pure angelic strain.
No more earth's fetters clog thy soul,
  Its aspirations be
E'en higher, holier, happier,
  Than we could ask for thee.
A gift is thine, a priceless gift.
  To mount on poet's wings,
Like a bird. that takes its upward flight
  To soar o'er earthly things.
Behold, with what a magic power
  In fancy's colors dressed,
Each treasured thought thou bring'st to light
  Which some could ne'er express.
Revealing oft the hidden source
  Of sorrow's secret sting,

That from our withered hopes, alas,
   Our dearest joys may spring.
If such thy power, O, greater far
   Must be thy spirit's need,
Now from the ashes of the past
   Let hope and joy proceed.
E'en though earth's shadows, thou
   Must pass, on to the eternal shore ;
How fearfully life's pilgrimage
   Is stretching on before!
Along thy path the clouds disperse,
   The shadows onward flee,
Yea; sweetly looking from above
   Thy Father smiling see.
Deep sorrows purify the heart,
   Meekly accept His grace ;
E'en smiling through the darkest cloud,
   Thou'lt see an angel's face,
Now helping thee to bear earth's ills
   With calm and patient grace.

TO H. M. H.

Marie we love thy gentle grace,
  So free from pride or art,
Uniting all those lovelier traits.
  So sure to win the heart.

Life hath its joys and sorrows, too,
  For spirits such as thine ;
Its highest, holiest purposes.
  Its sweetest hopes are thine.

With a clear perception of the good,
  The beautiful and true,
Invigorates the thirsting soul,
  As flowers inhale the dew.

Now, looking o'er the sunny past,
  Or onward as thou will,
Strong in thy conscious rectitude,
  Thou'lt rise above all ill.

While ministering kindly to the wants
  Of sickness or of age,
Or with a keen, inquiring glance,
  Scanning life's hidden page ;

Remembering, if the tempest lower,
  And earthly hopes are riven,
Enough, enough for thee to know
  Thy path leads up to heaven.

TO A YOUNG LADY.

So gayly commencing thy brilliant career,
Allured by the pleasures, which youth make so
    dear,
Rare blending of charms in thy features I trace,
A rare emanation of beauty and grace.
How joyous thy prospects! thy spirits how light!
Each newly-sought pleasure so fraught with de-
    light!
Life's glittering attractions, realities seem ;
Love's witchery enhancing thy spirit's young
    dream.
Each one in their turn, may thy spirit enthrall.
Not a dread of the future does thy happiness pall.
Ah! vain the illusion to shackle a mind
Richly treasured with knowledge ; a spirit so kind
Can scarcely glide on, should it face the rude
    blast,
But shrink from the sorrows through which it must
    pass:—
Go cherish those virtues, the charm of thy youth,
The lovely enchantment of goodness and truth ;
Of the rich garlands thy bright fancy weaves,
No flower of them all, such rich fragrance leaves.

JESUS AT THE WELL.

He was not without the human ;
    As He came to the cool well's brink,
And seeing there a woman
    He asked her to give Him a drink.

And she, in her light, bantering tone,
    Asks for a reason why ;
While he sits on the old curb-stone,
    Waiting for a reply.

" How is it that thou being a Jew
    Come asking drink of me,
A woman of Samaria who
    No dealings have with thee."

"O, didst thou but know the gift of God,
    And who is speaking thus to thee,
Then wouldst thou of thine own accord,
    Come asking drink of me."

Then glancing down the well so steep,
    This trouble she foresaw :
" The well is deep, so very deep,
    And you can nothing draw.

AUTUMN LEAVES.

Our Father Jacob dug this well,
  And watered his flocks here,
And it is said the Prophet's tell
  Messiah shall appear.

It must have been a joy methinks,
  To hear Him then exclaim :
That "whoso of this water drinks
  Will never thirst again."

Willing to act the better part
  And ready to receive,
She murmured gently, " Sir, thou art
  A Prophet I perceive."

He offered drink from no choice cup,
  Of new or rare device,
But a fount of water springing up
  Into everlasting life.

" Give me to drink," the woman cried
  With interest brimming o'er
" That all my wants may be supplied,
  And I may thirst no more."

Back to the city hastened she,
  Saying to the people " come and see
A man from whom nothing is hid,
  For he told me all I ever did."

THE TRANSFIGURATION.

That will be the grandest story
   Told in the ages yet to come,
Of the three caught up in glory
   With our Christ, the holy One.

How great was their amazement,
   When, brighter than the sun.
They saw those holy Ancients,
   With their shining armor on.

What did the mystic splendor,
   And the dazzling show betide,
Had the pearly gates up yonder
   Opened then their portals wide ?

And was this visitation,
   So radiant to the sight,
The Heralds of Salvation
   From Him who dwells in light ?

All with their mission glowing,
   Forth from the Courts above,
A luminous outpouring
   Of God's redeeming love.

And then the three together,
　　In converse did appear,
As if strengthening each other
　　With words of hope and cheer.

Filled with the regal splendor,
　　We hear them now exclaim,
Lost in delight and wonder,
　　"Oh, let us here remain!"

Then said Peter unto Jesus
　　"We'll build us tabernacles three,
One for Moses, and Elias,
　　And another one for Thee."

In this joyous reunion
　　Of the old time and the new,
They forgot their earthly mission
　　And the work they had to do.

Instantly we see what followed—
　　That which made them so rejoice.
They were by a cloud o'ershadowed
　　And they heard from Heaven a voice.

Saying, "This is my beloved
　　Son in whom I am well pleased."
He the Chosen One, and Loved,
　　One in whom ye have believed.

18

Did Angelic Hosts of Heaven
  Now their endless praise begin,
When they heard the mandate given
  " My Beloved, hear ye Him ? "

The intense fervor of their souls
  To fearfulness gave place,
And startled out of all control,
  They fell upon their face.

Then after his own fashion,
  When he would the lambs have fed,
With the tenderest compassion
  He said " Be ye not afraid."

Wholly lost in admiration
  Of this glorious retreat,
They must need some confirmation,
  Coming from the Mercy Seat.

When the visitants had vanished,
  And the light that round them shone,
They were equally astonished,
  Finding Jesus all alone.

When awakened from the vision,
  A new light upon them broke ;
They remembered He had spoken
  " As before man never spoke."

Thus we see the special fitness
  For a work so aptly done ;
They must be the special witness
  When the Father owned his Son.

Far beyond their comprehension
  Was the consciousness of loss,
From the mysteries of redemption.
  Or the glories of the Cross.

He had checked their vain ambition,
  Fraught with dreams of fame and wealth,
Pointing them to such conditions
  Wholly lifting out of self.

They saw not, that to consummate
  The end He had in view,
Of blood and flame, the trackless waste
  That he must travel through.

When our hearts are filled with rapture,
  In the ecstacy of bliss,
O'er the prospects of the future
  Even we may ask amiss.

The glowing visitants they met,
  Shed lustre on the name,
Of him who led them step by step
  Up to a higher plain.

At Calvary and Gethsemane
  Their hearts with grief were riven,
But lo, the stone is rolled away,
  And Christ their Lord is risen.

INSPIRATION.

As in life's rugged pathway
  On some high purpose bent,
When nerved to vigorous action,
  We dare the rough ascent.
When we attempt a conquest
  The victory is half won,
Since virtue owes her vigor
  To obstacles o'er come.
The warfare is not suffered,
  To engender fear and strife,
But to waken into action
  The dormant powers of life.
How often do we see
  The dull and plodding mind,

When roused to energy
  With vigorous action joined.
Progressing slow but surely
  Onward step by step
His awakened soul on high
  Attainments set.
While pressing forward to the mark,
  Ne'er wearied nor grown faint,
But so determined, bursts his bonds
  And soars beyond constraint.
So wonderful the perfect trust he feels.
  His greatest thought too simple to reveal,
O'er passion's raging gulf,
  Or threatening clouds that lower,
Faith throws her rainbow bridge
  Entwined with many a flower.
The soul exulting soars on self-poised wings
And bows in reverence to the King of Kings.
Enclosed within a rough and prickly shell,
We find concealed the nut we love so well.
It needs the keen, cold, biting, frosty air,
To crack the bur and leave the kernel bare.
For ought we know a rough exterior may
Contain a soul, whose oft illumined ray
Will light the future of life's hidden page,
And prove at once, the landmarks of the age.

ASPIRATIONS.

Wearily no longer linger,
   Earnest soul, go take thy rest,
Upward, onward, through soft azure,
   Soar to mansions of the blest.

Longing soul, why shouldst thou tarry,
   Now thy wings are plumed for flight?
Upward, onward, soar triumphant,
   On to realms of endless light.

Panting soul, no longer tarry,
   Earth would dim thy longings quite,
O'er the rosy tints of even
   Spreads the darker wing of night.

Fainting soul, no longer tarry,
   High attainments wouldst thou win?
Wouldst thou grasp thy bright ideal,
   Instantly thy work begin.

See, ah see! what dazzling splendor
   Streams along the milky way!
And the morning stars together
   Hymning their triumphant lay.

Wouldst thou up and join the chorus?
   O'er the stars wouldst thou have scope?
Bow adoring; upward soaring,
   Evermore rejoice and hope.

MISFORTUNE.

When smitten by the first great blow,
  The anguished soul lies prostrate, bleeding,
We think no other heart can know
  The anguish that our own is feeling.

In deep, impenetrable woe,
  'Neath the mighty conflict bending,
A pressure crushing us so low,
  O will there never be an ending ?

Some show in wild and fitful mood
  The waves of anguish tossing there,
While calmer souls, by grace subdued,
  Wrestle in patience with despair.

The stricken soul awakes at last
  From its dull, leaden weight of sorrow,
And, sighing o'er its struggles past,
  Clings to the promise of the morrow.

For hope, tho' dimmed, is never gone,
  Her angel wing is hovering o'er us,
And still alluring further on,
  Is ever ready to enfold us.

A higher bliss the soul receives,
　　When looking from its earthly prison.
Through clouds and darkness, it perceives
　　A shining pathway up to heaven.

There surging sorrows sweetly rest,
　　Hushed in the breathings of a prayer ;
Hope enters, a delightful guest,
　　And, joyous, takes possession there.

The soothing virtue it imparts,
　　The canker worm of grief destroys,
And opens up within the heart
　　A well-spring of perpetual joys.

FAITH.

Can we doubt of a hereafter
　When we cry in accents wild,
Father hear me, oh my Father!
　He will own and bless his child.

Loss or gain for nothing counting,
　Gone the fear of care and strife,
For the soul is upward mounting,
　Soaring upward into life.

Fount of love, the living essence,
　Peace and joy to us impart,
Filling with thy living presence
　Every nook of this poor heart.

O the joy of this indwelling,
　To the heart that's cleansed from sin,
All the mysteries revealing
　Of the hidden life within.

THE YOUNG RULER.

We read that on a certain day,
　There was among the throng

Of followers that passed that way,
  As Jesus came along,
A suppliant with ability,
  Who, kneeling at His feet,
In tones of deep humility,
  His mercy did entreat.

He was a noble, rich, young jew
  Who sought the pearl of price ;
" Good master, pray what shall I do
  To inherit eternal life? "
" Why callest thou me good ?
  But One good thou may'st call,
And He is God, our Father,
  Creator of us all."

" Thou knowest the commands,
  And how they must be kept,
Including all the law demands,
  Owe no man any debt."
He answered "I have loved the truth,
  And honored each precept,
All the commandments from my youth
  I zealously have kept."

To an approving mind
  His highest aims were reached,

But from this interview we find
　His troubles were increased.
But in his heart far out of sight,
　Was many a little shoot,
Which, never having seen the light,
　As yet had borne no fruit.

Discerning in this hidden graft,
　The thing that he must flee,
His master said, " sell what thou hast
　And come and follow me."
The highest bliss, a joy sublime,
　Could this young ruler see ;
This invitation given in time,
　Was for eternity.

With spotless record in the past,
　And wealth an ample store,
With his possession all so vast,
　He needed one thing more.
Christ offered bliss without alloy ;
　His eye on him had shone ;
If he would have supernal joy
　The choice must be his own.

How sorrowful he turned away !
　Sighs mingled with regret ;

When he heard the blessed master say,
　　" One thing thou lackest yet ;
Let thy heart be the open door,
　　Of all thy goods possessed
Distribute freely to the poor,
　　And thou shalt gain the rest."

What cause was here for mental strife,
　　In this which he now must do !
Upsetting all his plans in life,
　　And beginning them anew.
He was bidden to surrender
　　All his valued earthly means,
And become a lowly follower
　　Of the hated Nazarene.

We may learn in the hereafter
　　All this suffering denotes,
For the wishes of the master
　　Were the death knell to his hopes.
His selfishness had taken root ;
　　And love's diviner ray,
Though flooding him from head to foot,
　　Could not the mischief stay.

Plenty and ease enough thro' life
　　His longing heart to fill :

And he would ease this mental strife,
　By a persistent will.
We find not in the written word,
　The depths of his remorse,
Or what relentless furies raged
　Over his unkempt hearth.

We know not if sin held control,
　Or how or when or where
The hidden anguish of his soul
　Yielded to dark despair.
Faith gives the assurance that we may
　Lean on his staff and rod,
And find that the impossible with man,
　Is possible with God.

And of the poor lame man, we read,
　Who came and could do no more,
So many pressing on ahead,
　And stepping down before.
For in his dire extremity
　This lame man it appears,　.
Suffered from an infirmity,
　Full eight and thirty years.

That law of nature they obeyed,
　Who came in search of health,

And by no hindrances were stayed,
　　But each one for himself.
The eager crowd are hurrying down
　　Impatient of delay,
When the despondents wish to crown,
　　The Saviour came that way.

Seeing this poor man in such a guise,
　　What pity filled his soul,
He spoke to him without disguise
　　Saying, wilt thou be made whole?
He manifested no surprise
　　As he heard the poor man talk,
Then saying unto him, arise,
　　Take up thy bed, and walk. ·

One word has changed the sufferer's lot,
　　The stricken limbs are free,
As the waters sprang from Marah's rock
　　Or healing from the tree.
For the instruction of the hour
　　Which no man might gainsay
He manifested forth his power,
　　Then left without delay.

He knew that on that very day
　　Whatever might betide,

Levite and Priest were on the way
  To spread dissension wide.
As the Saviour hastened from the spot,
  Careless of praise or blame,
They railed on him for caring not
  The Sabbath to profane.

Then, meeting Jesus at the porch,
  Where he had gone before,
He said to him, beware henceforth
  And go and sin no more.

FRIENDSHIP.

I gave thee in my youth,
  With feelings pure and warm,
A friendship based on truth,
  Which nothing might disarm.

A friendship formed in youth
  From tastes pure and refined,
Promised a larger growth
  Than lures the common mind.

How oft we gathered them,—
  The rarest flowers we sought,,
And many a hidden gem
  From the sweet pearls of thought.

Thy trials but ennobled thee,
  Thou wast so true and kind,
In this cold world we rarely see
  A more exalted mind.

And still the passing years,
  Found thee enjoying health ;
And better than thy fears,
  Possessing joy and wealth.

Nobly thou stood the test,
  A very little while,
And was thyself possessed
  With the same glad smile.

But soon the wary sought
  Thy faltering steps to guide,
In fashion's dizzy maze they thought
  Thou wert all untried.

Grandly thou stood the restless din
  With a sad, scornful smile,
But step by step was hurried in
  Like a bewildered child.

For fashion hath her gilded shrine
  Which claims obeisance now,
And if her votaries would shine,
  They must before it bow.

But now thou art so changed,
  One scarce can brook
The calm, but cold and strange
  Indifference of thy look.

For as the heart grows cold,
  And gentler thoughts erased,
Time will at last unfold
  A pure, warm soul, debased.

Take back, take back the gift,
  Thou hast so lightly bore,
I may not value it
  Since it is prized no more.

The bitter lesson learned,
  By such sad experience taught,
Had been too dearly earned,
  Although so cheaply bought.

A. D. MERRILL.

[Published by request.]

And when I think of Abraham D.,
A faith-illumined face I see ;
For even I, nor was I alone,
Discerned in him a face that shone.

Glowing as if some radiant morn
He caught a glimpse of saints upborne,
And that sufficed that lurid ray
To light them on their heavenward way.

Halting at times on sunny heights,
Gained only by aerial flights,
And seeing oft the rosy flush,
As Moses did in the burning bush.

And deemed not of the afterglow,
Whatever from such contacts flow,
And he did sing, yes, he did sing
Like the rapt bird upon the wing.

Well known as one faithful and true,
Who sought his Master's work to do ;
He gladly trod life's rugged road,
Cheating its cares of half their load,

Strong in the faith, his ear was quick
To hear the suffering of the sick,
And by the sweetness of his strain,
Soothed the intensity of pain.

Once there, he would both sing and pray,
And talk of heaven and show the way,
Teaching them of a faith sublime
That leads the soul to heavenward clime.

Leading church service, he would sing
Like the rapt bird upon the wing.
Till the voices of the mighty host
In one grand chorus borne aloft,
In strains that made the echoes ring,
With boundless praise to heaven's high King.

EGG ROCK.

Egg Rock, if thou art so lonely now,
Uplifting heavenward thy lofty brow,
'Neath the warm radiance of a sunny sky,
Thy calm, still beauty delights the eye
When seemingly, as if in sportive play,

The sparkling wave throws up its foamy spray,
Or creeping on, only to backward flee,
Chasing each other in the wildest glee,
And then in softened murmur's lullaby
In mournful cadence, with the sea bird's cry.
Firm and erect, thou seem'st to say with pride,
Behold me beaming o'er the ocean wide ;
But if beneath a summer's smiling sky
Thy charming scenery so delights the eye,
When all the waiting isles, the sea, the air,
Is wafting to Heaven, the incense of prayer,
And in low monotones old ocean sings,
Her deep toned anthem to the King of kings ;
Who holds the helm, and who alone presides,
Who rules the storms, and on the ocean rides,
O how majestic, when the raging sea
Its threat'ning billows, rushes upon thee,
And wildly dashing on, shock after shock,
Repelled by thee, thou adamantine rock,
Vainly the billows, rear their lofty crest
Like angry demons driven to unrest.
In thundering gusts, along thy rocky strand
Its deafening roar so fearful to withstand,
Thou like a monarch on his natal day,
Obedient only to the Almighty sway,
Undaunted stand, holding aloft thy light—
Guiding the mariner on his way aright.

Thro' storms and darkness send thy cheering ray
A beacon light for ships that pass that way,
Their sole dependence on His sovereign will,
Who to the angry waves, said, " Peace be still."

THE CARIBOU QUEEN.

Now there came unto a region wild
A father with his only child ;
Standing aloof from all—you could see
In his bearing some dark mystery.

He took up a grant, and staked off his claim
Without so much as giving his name,
And he was so reticent, no one dared
To intrude upon him unawares.

Without introduction of some sort—
Fearing there might be a sharp retort,—
His child, a girl of sweet sixteen,
Preserved the same cold, haughty mien.

But the lithe damsel on her part
Seemed to be one of the pure in heart;
Modest and retiring to that degree
That for them she would be no company.

He built his cabin on the lot
In a little more secluded spot,
Where the wealth of nature could impart
What they might never gain from art.

Where, with his child, he would reside
Shut out from all the world beside.
Sometimes in a little shady nook
She was seen with her pencil or a book ;

For she was one whose chief delight,
Was from reveling in fancy's flight :
Here culture left, with talents rare,
Resources now beyond compare.

What else could o'er her life's calm flow
In roseate hues, its colors glow,
Investing all the hills and wood,
With a charm that to her mind is food.

And it was soon whispered round his claim
That from America he came ;
And from his indifference he won
The sobriquet of "old Caribou."

Now it so happens in the range
There is always something for a change ;—
A bird, a flower, or a little child,
Would almost set the maiden wild.

Such little ones she'd gather round,—
As in the camp are sometimes found—
And from her kindness won, it would seem,
The title of " The Caribon Queen."

With no diversion of any sort,
He kept steadily on his routine of work,
Deeper and deeper delving on,
With what success was never known.

And now there happened something strange,
A rich young nobleman came to the range,
Seeking rather abroad to roam
Than to stay in his palatial home.

It was this young man's happy fate
To be sole heir of a great estate ;
His mother dying when he was young,
Sir Charles left all to his only son.

Sir Charles possessed with winning grace,
A noble form, and faultless face,
And withal a charm of mind,
With ease and dignity combined.

Now it happened in this family of theirs,
They were singularly destitute of heirs,
But the few remaining with high birth,
Were blest with culture and mental worth.

His title, estates, and family pride,
With all the distinction which it implied ;
Were I to attempt, my pen would fail
To describe the splendor of "Heathdale."

The imposing mansion, stood on ground
For many acres stretched around,
The landscape gardening in device :—
It was called a perfect paradise.

And when his ancestors did there reside,
The name was symbolic of honor and pride ;
And he with a perfect form and face
Had all the intelligence of his race.

Honors at Oxford, creditably won,
Precedence given to his father's son ;
But scarcely had his honors been received,
E'er by his father's death he was bereaved.

Now, reinstated master of "Heathdale"
According to the order of entail,
From this time forth, as we can say,
Sir Charles had it his own way.

For hail'd with acclamations, on every side,
Not long with any party to preside,
For when professors have done their best,
O then, society must do the rest.

When the precedence is given to the upper ten
Of beautiful women and polished men ;
When at the banquet and the ball,
And stately dames, at fashion's call

Came to the concert and the play,
And dance and sing the night away ;
When celebrities all give their shout
And the " reigning stars are trotted out."

For here society, it would seem,
Was found the " *creme de la creme.*"
Sir Charles being of a nature rare and fine ;
Held his honors by right divine.

Being so thoughtful, it was his fate
To be received everywhere with joy elate ;
And scheming mothers were sorely tried,
When they saw their snares all set aside.

Tired of the banquets, and the balls,
Given in his old ancestral halls,
Tired of the revels and the feast,
Which never satifies in the least ;

21

Tired of the concert and the play,
And the trivial pleasures of the day,
Tired of emulation, and the strife
That emanates from such a life,—

Where men of letters and of fame,
And all the other celebrities came ;
Some to bolster their family pride
By securing at once, a wealthy bride.

For many a gay young millionaire
Is taken by the thoughtless debonair,
Caring more for such foolish trifles
That are attached to empty titles.

But young Sir Charles shut up the old hall,
And closed his doors to one and all.
The next we hear, has started on his way
Across the ocean, to America.

And after that, going at the usual rates
Of travelling, all over the States.
He joined the hunting party roving round,
Next we find him on the Selkirk ground.

Sir Charles dropped his titles and identity,
Joining this jovial young company,
Neglecting the claims of home and friend—
Not a word of his whereabouts did he send.

But the camp-fires blazed up every night,
With such happy faces glowing in their light ;
While they relate such thrilling wild tales
To secure the interest which never fails.

Showing their own peculiar knack
Of taking the buffalo herds in their track ;
Or the trappings used in pretense to snare
The cunning beaver out from his lair.

The mirth and song, with the festal cheer,
And the saddle, kept him about three years ;
Then eschewing the bolder huntsman's horn,
He awoke at the Caribon range one morn.

Our hero like many an one of his kind,
Needed something to settle his mind,
And hears with an interest we have foreseen
The story of the young Caribon queen.

That her father severely taxed his strength ;
Nor suffering his child to go her length,
And she so gentle, true and good,
Did up the work and prepared his food.

And they spoke of her as one supreme,—
Beautiful as a poet's dream,
Whose golden ringlets like a veil
Over her shapely shoulders fell.

There was but one since she came to the west,
And he seemed to her the noblest, the best,
And he had taxed his wits the while,
To gain from her a passing smile.

Offering his sympathy to this poor, old man,
And such meagre excuses as he could plan,
To gain an entrance to that little home,
Where no one was ever allowed to come.

Still more alluring was his charm of mind,
With dignity of manner so combined,
His elegance and wondrous power to please,
So engaging when combined with social ease.

That old Caribon at last was fairly won,
Not only he, for it was not he alone,
A rarer flush stole o'er her cheek,
And seldom could she trust her voice to speak.

Blanched to whiter hue his once brown hair;
Tugged at his heart the vulture of despair.
His nerves seemed to be hung on wires,
The lightning flash of internal fires.

Must he leave this dearly loved, innocent child
Alone in this drear and rugged wild,
No one to love her, and to protect,
Or from whom she could a ray of comfort get?

From her social position and high birth,
He had dragged her down almost to earth,
Even now her footsteps gently glide
Away from his bed, her grief to hide.

Had she not caught a heavenly ray
From her mother on her dying day,
Pointing her upward to the sky
Where she would meet her by and by.

As age grew on apace, tempering his desire,
And quenching at its source the fire
Of youth, which, like a rushing tide,
Urges its victim on in hasty stride.

So this strange man, in agony and shame
Writhed over the dishonor to his name,
A vain ambition lured him to the verge
Where avarice ceased not her claim to urge.

And now death was staring him in the face,
With the endless torment of his disgrace,
Without the power to make amends,
He was driven out from home and friends.

Her father thinking over in his mind,
Seeming at last to grow resigned :
Bade them come in manner so brief
That it really seemed to be a relief.

Seeing what in the event was proved,
That by his presence she was moved ;
And at the mention of his name
A change over her spirit came.

As he struggles for returning peace,
Her filial piety and tenderness increase :
And so increase his reverence and love
That angels might look on from above.

Yet even now every wit was taxed
Ere to a smile her features would relax,
But even this his love could not disarm,
It drew him on and so increased the charm.

Old Caribon feeling the end must come,
And that by penitence heaven might be won,
No longer o'er past splendors sighed,
But sought the peace of the sanctified.

Of grasping minions he had been the tool,
And while aping the excess of fools,
The demons of his fate each nobler purpose
    dodged,
And petted minions sat in state where angels
    might have lodged.

And now before him such visions glide ;
The wife who was once his joy and pride,
And his splendid mansion was all ablaze
With music and light of other days.

Again whirled on in the ceaseless rounds
Where false ambition knows no bounds,
Till, as in a glass he saw it was all ;
Like a species of madness his senses fall.

The winter daily growing more severe
Offered no hope this old man's heart to cheer,
His hardships had so worn upon his frame,
That o'er him a childlike weakness came.

Fever set in :—fearing it might be the end,
She sent to Sir Charles as to their only friend ;
He found her kneeling at the old man's side,
Striving in vain her o'ermastering grief to hide.

Sir Charles seeing there must be no delay
Offered to marry her that very day,
And with a noble bearing firm and free
Frankly disclosing his identity.

And motioning her aside, too weak to call,
Her father said to her, tell him all.
He was president of a San Francisco bank,
One of the wealthiest companies extant.

Going beyond the laws of life's social walks,
Unwisely led to speculate in stocks,
And downward, step by step, was foolishly led,
Until as a defaulter he had fled.

Lost his integrity and betrayed his trust,
Lured by temptation for the golden dust,
The gathering mist had onward rolled
Till he was quite enveloped in its folds.

When forced his infamy there to explain,
A sudden trembling seized her frame,
Seeing, he clasped her in a warm embrace
Saying the grave would bury the disgrace.

A missionary in the camp being notified,
Straightway the nuptial knot is tied.
Her father feeling heaven at last had smiled
By bestowing this protector on his child.

He had not married a dowerless bride,
Succeeding revelations verified
His treasure bags were filled to excess
With golden nuggets more or less.

SEQUEL TO THE CARIBOU QUEEN.

Now it seems proper to relate
The sequel to Sir Charles's fate,
How, that finding enough to do in the main,
He concluded to stay and settle the claim.

Within the week the old gentleman died,
Clinging to the faith of the crucified ;
They buried him there in a shady dell,
And over him a vail of silence fell.

He built a house where he might reside
In comfort with his beautiful bride,
She, believing in him with her whole soul,
Left everything to his control.

Now we read the miners seeking more gain,
Resolved on selling out at the range.
A year had passed ere he made the sale,
And a little heir was born to " Heathdale."

We see a life of faith and trust,
Exert an influence as it must,
There has never been such rejoicing since,
As hailed the birth of the little prince.

22

As she stood with her beautiful babe in her arms,
Softened grace enhanced her charms;
An expression, it seems lent from above
To show the depths of a mother's love.

Sir Charles had gone down into the mine
To settle things for the last time,
When to their horror and surprise
The mine caved in and buried him alive.

Down so deep under the ground,
That his poor body never was found;
Seemed almost too sad to relate,
This passage in his mournful fate.

Now picture the anguish that on her fell,
As they go to her and the story tell,
Or saw when the fearful tidings came,
The distress and sorrow that shook her frame.

How terrible to the young wife,
Crushing out all her hopes of life,
No longer wishing abroad to roam,
He had made up his mind to take her home.

For hope in future there is no room,
And all is shrouded in sadness and gloom,
Left in the world friendless and alone,
But for this babe, her heart was stone.

How many were the hours to memory given,
Recalling joys ere now that seemed like heaven ;
Now what we read does not seem strange,
She with her babe has left the range.

The agents having got some clue,
Are out searching the region through,
For the mother and child, who without fail
Are the rightful heirs of the estate of "Heathdale."

KOSSUTH.

Lo! on a pilgrimage to our blest land,
For the oppressed, a Kossuth bravely stands.
A wandering exile o'er life's rough sea ;
From home and friends and country forced to flee.

Borne on the heaving billows' surging breast,
To freedom's shore, a welcome, honored guest.
All hail to thee, thou wise and mighty chief ;
Noble in all, but greater in thy grief.

Still on thy God, most humbly dost thou wait ;
Thy soul unconquered by its mournful fate ;
As much superior in thy strength of mind,
As the forest tree, that towers above its kind.

Rising from stern oppression's iron heel,
Thy cruel wrongs our people deeply feel.
O'er all the earth the mighty evils brood,
Which must be counteracted by the good.

In souls content, ambition finds no home,
Driven from the cot, it lurks behind the throne.
Add throne to throne ; extend the vast empire ;
The thirst increases with enlarged desire.

In proof of this, what greater would ye have
Than all the mighty masters of the age ?
Napoleon, who in his triumphal hour,
Stood forth a giant of colossal power.

At once the pride and glory of all lands ;
More conquered yet than conquerors he stands,
Since that lone exile to his sea-girt rock,
Relieved the nations of a sudden shock.

Their tired energies have sought repose,
Proud of their triumph o'er their haughty foes.
And since the fearful menaces have ceased,
Wealth and prosperity have much increased.

Self-satisfied perhaps, but not forsooth,
For any love of justice and of truth ;
But as the fierce tiger coolly licks each wound,
Ere making ready for another bound,

Just so this seeming quiet all the while,
Produced an issue very dark and vile.
Portentious is the coming of that night,
Whose gathering clouds so much obscure the light.

While lurid flashes lighten all the sky,
Showing the frightful tempest is so nigh.
While rain, and hail, in fitful gusts rush past,
Like maddened furies driven by the blast.

And muttering thunders growing yet more loud,
Discharge the contents of the angry cloud.
And when the elemental strife shall cease,
A heavenly calm broods o'er ; and all is peace.

And when at last the blissful change appears,
It raises hope, and scatters all our fears.
The rich abundance of the soil
Amply repays the laborer for his toil.

Much has been done within the shortest space,
Toward lifting up the fallen of our race,
And earnest efforts must be ever made,
To raise man's aims to a higher grade.

Why so much evil lurks amidst the good,
Is easier to be seen than can be understood.
While science for her part, no light upon it throws,
And genius isn't able the answer to disclose.

But all the myst'ries which are so concealed,
In coming time, to us will be revealed,
In sunshine of God's smile, the truth will then have
        birth ;
While knowledge of our Lord shall cover all the
        earth.

IN MEMORIAM.

[B. F. ALLEY.]

It was but a few short days,
    We scarce had turned about,
Since last we saw him,
    Passing in and out.
Glowing so fair and fresh,
    With every living grace

His soul's best attributes.
   Seen on his speaking face.
His grand and noble form,
   His majesty of mien,
Commanding reverence
   Wherever he was seen.
His seeming strength,
   His firm, elastic tread,
To years of usefulness
   Our teeming fancy led.
If life be measured by the amount
Of duties entered in account,
And strength of purpose to fulfil,
In obedience to our Father's will,
Then he was standing on safe ground,
And always at his post was found
Engaged in all that was good and true,
Ready his Master's work to do.
He must have been one of God's own,
On whom the star of Bethlehem shone
A ray divine out from the heavenly zone,
By faith illumined on his pathway shone,
Leading him on to mansions of the blest,
To him who giveth his beloved rest.

REV. DANIEL FILMORE.

[By request.]

Now Mr. Filmore as a man
Impressed me, as no other can ;
His words so gentle, kind and true,
Fell from his lips distilled like dew.
He looked like one who unawares
Had wrestled on invisible stairs,
Or by the touch of angel's wings,
Gave evidence of unseen things.

And ever after, bore the trait
Of having seen an angel's face:
This inspiration from above
Was seen in nameless acts of love.
Urging them even to accord,
That reverence to his holy word,
Who sits like a refiner's fire
Purging from every low desire.

He lived for God, not for a name,
And never dreamed of empty fame ;
He taught a faith whose crystal ray
Transmutes the darkness into day.
The faith which led the Patriarch on
When Abram offered up his son;
The faith in which their souls were tried;
The faith in which they lived and died.

JESUS AT THE POOL.

From o'er Judea's rugged hills,
    And down its sunny slopes,
There came the voice of one that thrills
    And elevates man's hopes.

Capernaum in thy borders round,
    What lessons there were taught,
Within thy very sight and sound,
    What mighty wonders wrought.

The waves were stilled at his command,
    While devils onward flee,
And just as safely as on land
    He walks upon the sea.

    Then Jesus came unto the pool,
    Its waters oft so calm and cool,
    Where by a special act of grace,
    An angel moved upon its face ;
    Healing disease of every kind :—
    The lame, the impotent and blind.
    Who would its efficacy prove,
    Must step in when the waters move.

AN ACROSTIC.

Let your thoughts ever turn to that
 Final goal,
Upward and onward the home
 Of the soul.
Each bright aspiration serves but
 To increase
Love's shining attendants, Faith, Hope,
 Joy and Peace.
Like the incense of praise to the fond
 Mother's heart,
A glow with a fervor that will
 Never depart;
Giving no room for error or doubt
 On thy part.
Each day bears a record of goodness
 And truth,
Richly laden with sheaves, garnered
 Up in thy youth.
Rich lessons of wisdom, unfolding
 In love,
Your faith looking up to the
 Mansions above.

TO SARAH.

So fair in life's first opening morn,
A flower thou seemest without a thorn,
Rapt in its folds, who would suppose
An opening bud the worm enclosed.
How cunningly it lies concealed,
Kindly the sunbeams warmth revealed.
In vain the tender flowers thou'll nurse,
No more it will thrive, but droops to earth.
Gaily before thee in their pride.
Mere phantoms of beauty will often glide,
And flattering smile, if not too late,
Now think sweet *love*, of the rosebud's fate.
How, carelessly flinging in all their worth
And richness, thy young affections forth,
Yea, trust not too fondly, nor think it strange,
Does a passing breath, their fresh hues change.
Earth's fleeting joys too soon you'll find
Ne'er satisfied the immortal mind.

MY ROSE.

It was a modest plant ;
　　It had both sun and shade,
No care it seem'd to want
　　In the sweet soil, where it laid.
A fine and healthy shrub,
　　Quite rapidly it grew,
All rich in clustering buds,
　　And blossoms not a few.

I said of buds and flowers,
　　There surely will be some,
To cheer the wintry hours ;
　　When brighter ones are gone.
Nourished by the fresh dews,
　　And the soft, cooling showers,
It promises to outdo
　　All the rich summer flowers.

But soon my little plant,
　　Sunshine and showers defied ;
And while no care it seemed to want,
　　Withered away and died.
And while I watched each leaf
　　And every little shoot,
Had never thought that underneath
　　A worm was at the root.

And, when I looked about
  This world so bright and fair,
What evils might be rooted out
  If each one did their share :
By seeking out the hidden germ
  That lurks in secret nooks,
And help the unwary ones to learn
  This mischief at the roots.

Within the haunts of sin and vice,
  What misery and woe,
Avoided by the warning voice
  Ere they descend so low.
Could they be brought to feel,
  And their downward path to trace,
And see that right upon the heel
  Death stares them in the face.

THE OAK AND THE VINE.

More than all the rest combined
I wondered at those climbing vines,
That creeping on from tree to tree
Had twined them in, so carelessly.

And not contented yet, we find
Had fastened on an aged pine,
Ah vainly mayest thou sigh and fret,
For thou art fairly taken in my net.

Then bounding o'er a brave old oak
It never a vine or tendril broke,
Ah vain thy struggles to be free,
Henceforth my prisoner thou must be.

But here we must not linger long.
For still the vine is creeping on,
Securely swinging at its ease
And rocked by every passing breeze.

Showing that youth and age entwin'd
Life's rough ascents may safely climb,
And meeting oft, shake hands at last,
O'er the frightful gulfs that they have passed.

While rich in fruits they thus recline,
The aged oak and youthful vine,
The weaker saplings, as they ought
Fling out their tendrils for support.

And vine and limb together droop,
So heavily laden with their fruit,
Well ripened now, the eye to win
And ready to be gathered in.

LOUISE.

Not quite a year since she had taken
  The bridal wreath from off her brow,
Then at its final consummation
  She breathed the marriage vow.

For love and joy had left such traces
  Of gladness on a brow so fair,
I doubted not that all the graces
  Had met in conclave there.

Leaving such a heavenly impress,
  On her sweet, angelic face,
Being in herself loves witness,
  That time can ne'er efface.

And I doubted not, the angels
  Watching o'er her from above,
Must approve the sweet evangel
  Of such innocence and love.

It had been her sweet vocation,
  To care for such dear little ones,
As engaged the approbation
  Of Him who bade them come.

So faithfully she did her part
  To the little ones enrolled,
Drawing them gently to her heart
  With such a sweet control.

And she, so rich in happiness,
  With a wealth of love, had come
To endow with all this tenderness
  And grace, another's home.

So endeared by this relation,
  Of a wife to the one she loved,
And secure in his affection,
  Her constancy she proved.

In the dawning of the morning,
  Ere she was summoned to depart,
She did press a tender life bud,
  Pressed it to her quivering heart.

Precious babe, the last sweet token,
  Of a full heart's overflow,
Ne'er thy name by her be spoken,
  Ne'er a mother's love to know.

She had lavished love on others,
  Soothing them to peaceful rest,
Now it must be by another,
  Her own little one is blest.

Never to feel the sweet reliance,
  In a mother's love possessed,
Never in love's gentle dalliance,
  Will her lips to thine be pressed.

Never to see the beaming love light,
  Shining in her soft dark eye,
When the happy little sprite,
  Springs to papa, standing by.

O say, dear friend, is it not better
  For you to meet her in the home above ?
Would you the immortal spirit fetter,
  With this frail blossom of an earthly love ?

No, rather follow on to those bright mansions,
  The place the Saviour promised to prepare,
Where seraph-like in glorious expansion,
  She is waiting to receive you there.

Farewell, Louise, a light breaks o'er the gloom,
  An arm of strength has borne thy spirit up,
Illumining thy pathway to the tomb,
  How else could you have tasted of death's bit-
    ter cup.

No gathering mist can ever intervene,
  To dim the brilliance of thy cloudless sky ;
For up, far up, beyond this earthly scene,
  Swings ope the pearly gates of paradise.

24

Thy gentle voice, whose flute like tones
　To silence hushed life's fears and strife,
Makes melody in that blest zone,
　With saints around the tree of life.

And as dust to dust is reunited,
　And life and immortality is thine,
May this pure ray that was on the altar lighted
　Shed its hallowed influence on fond memory's
　　• shrine.

WEEDS.

These lines were suggested by reading an article on the peculiari-
ty of weeds by Dr. McMillan in the Magazine.

———

Say, is it not a very curious thing
That from man's toil the weeds do spring?
That which makes it even worse,
Is that it springs from Adam's curse.

God said to Adam while in Paradise,
Because thou hast harkened to thy wife,
And instead of listening unto me,
Hast eaten of the forbidden tree.

Now cursed is the ground all for thy sake,
In sorrow of thy bread thou shalt partake,
Thorns and thistles it shall bring forth to thee,
Because thou hast eaten of the forbidden tree.

Weeds never have been found on virgin soil,
Where with the plough, man does not toil,
For it seems where're the ground is broke,
The weeds spring forth at every stroke.

They never seem to be in haste,
On the wild uncultivated waste;
On the high slopes are never seen,
Though mosses carpet them with green.

Where'er you see a rich corn field,
The thistle an abundance yields ;
Sheep's sorrel is found in the potato-plot
And around every barnyard lot.

And when you plant the garden seed,
Forth comes the groundsel and chickweed ;
In vain you'll try the unwelcome guest to dodge
They are sure to find a place somewhere to lodge.

Down to the meadow hie for flag or duck
For winter laying up a little stock.
The dandelion springs where man resides,
Spotting with golden blossoms, the waysides.

Its light and downy seeds float on the air,
Alight and germinating, spring up there ;
And ragwort is found in many a spot
With heartsease, tansy and burdock,

Mustard springs up so wild and free,
Its spoken of in scripture as a tree,
We think of them as troublesome weeds,
Forgetting the virtue of their seeds.

And if with thistles overgrown,
Who would the prickly weeds disown.
That has ever seen its downy ball,
With milkweed and dried grasses all ;

Or ever give up the flushy plume
That from the dried milkpods exhume.
The whip with nine lashes or cat-o'nine-tails,
To attract the attention, never fails.

It might seem folly, so to speak
Of Aaron's rod, or the house leek,
And if horseradish seems to invite,
You may always test it by the bite.

In the Arctic, and Antartic zone,
Such things as weeds are never known :
In Australia or America they were not found,
Now in abundance they abound.

For in no case can it be true,
That man can nothing find to do ;
So long as in the world around,
He can cultivate and till the ground.

www.ingramcontent.com/pod-product-compliance
Lightning Source LLC
Chambersburg PA
CBHW022352020726
47500CB00002B/239